Maureen Burke danced

Throwing herself into this pocket of time, matching the steps of this leanly athletic man with charismatic blue eyes and a sexual intensity as potent as his handsome face.

Brains. Brilliance. A body to die for and a loyal love of family.

Xander Lourdes was a good man.

But not her man. Only her boss.

And too soon, her work visa was due to expire. And officials had thus far denied her requests to extend it. She would have to go home to Ireland. To face all she'd run from, to leave this amazing place.

So Maureen breathed in the salty air mixed with the scent of burning wood from the bonfire and allowed herself to be swept away by the dance. By the look of this man with coal-black hair that spiked with the sea breeze and a hint of sweat. His square jaw was peppered with a five-o'clock shadow, his shoulders broad in his tuxedo, broad enough to carry the weight of the world.

Shivering with warm tingles that had nothing to do with any bonfire or humid night, she felt the attraction radiating off him the same way it heated her. She'd sensed the draw before, but his grief was so well-known she hadn't wanted to wade into those complicated waters.

Maureen wasn't interested in a relationship, but maybe if she was leaving she could indulge...

* * *

The Boss's Baby Arrangement is part of Harlequin Desire's #1 bestselling series, Billionaires and Babies: Powerful men...wrapped around their babies' little fingers.

Dear Reader,

I *am* an animal rescuer. It's not something I *do*. It's who I *am*. For years, I've been active in volunteering at local shelters, but only in the past couple of years realized the time had come to be a part of starting a 501(c)(3) animal rescue. Little did I realize what an exciting, overwhelming, sometimes heartbreaking, but ultimately rewarding adventure that would be.

Needless to say, my work in animal rescue and my years in Florida inspired *The Boss's Baby Arrangement*. A long drive through the magnificently exotic Florida Keys had me quickly convinced I absolutely had to set some stories there. And from that came the idea for the Lourdes Brothers of Key Largo, a family dedicated to saving and expanding a Florida wildlife preserve.

As my fingers flew across the keyboard, I soon found the animals weren't the only wild creatures to be found in Key Largo! I hope you enjoy the sexy Lourdes brothers and each man's journey to find the right woman.

Cheers,

www.CatherineMann.com

CATHERINE MANN

THE BOSS'S BABY ARRANGEMENT

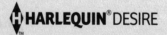

ISBN-13: 978-0-373-73481-8

The Boss's Baby Arrangement

Copyright © 2016 by Catherine Mann

Printed in U.S.A.

HARLEQUIN®
www.Harlequin.com

USA TODAY bestseller and RITA® Award winner **Catherine Mann** has penned over fifty novels, released in more than twenty countries. After years as a military spouse bringing up four children, Catherine is now a snowbird—sorta—splitting time between the Florida beach and somewhat chillier beach in her home state of South Carolina. The nest didn't stay empty long, though, as Catherine is an active board member for the Sunshine State Animal Rescue. www.CatherineMann.com

Books by Catherine Mann

Harlequin Desire

The Boss's Baby Arrangement
A Christmas Baby Surprise
Sheltered by the Millionaire

Diamonds in the Rough

One Good Cowboy
Pursued by the Rich Rancher
Pregnant by the Cowboy CEO

The Alpha Brotherhood

An Inconvenient Affair
All or Nothing
Playing for Keeps
Yuletide Baby Surprise
For the Sake of Their Son

Bayou Billionaires

His Pregnant Princess Bride
Reunited with the Rebel Billionaire

Visit her Author Profile page at Harlequin.com, or catherinemann.com, for more titles.

To Jeanette Vigliotti, a brilliant professor and a dear friend. So happy you are an unofficial part of our family!

One

Xander Lourdes had loved and lost his soul mate.

Parked in an Adirondack chair by the Gulf waters, he knew deep in his gut he wouldn't find that again. Even after a year, his wife's death from an aneurysm cut Xander to the core, but he'd been working like hell to find solace as best he could in honoring her memory every way possible.

By parenting their baby girl.

And by revitalizing a wildlife refuge in his dead wife's beloved Florida Keys. He'd invested half of his personal fortune to revitalize this place. No great hardship as far as the executive angle went. He thrived on that part.

Although the fundraising parties? Like tonight? The endless schmoozing? A real stick in the eye.

His preferred way to spend an evening was with his daughter, Rose, or in the office. These social gatherings tried his patience. For a moment his mind wandered back to how his wife had always stabilized and smoothed functions like this for him. She'd been a natural complement for him.

For his wife's memory, he endured the beachside gala.

Xander drank tonic water, half listening to the state politician rambling beside him about a childhood pet parakeet. Small talk had never been Xander's thing.

Waves crashed on the shore and a bonfire crackled at the high-end outdoor fundraiser. Tiki torch flames flickered, reaching toward the starlit sky as a steel-drum band played. Marshes *swooshed* with softer sounds in the distance, grasses and nocturnal creatures creating a night ensemble all their own.

A lengthy buffet table and bar kept the partygoers well stocked by the waitstaff currently weaving through the crowd of partiers talking or dancing barefoot on the sand, silk and diamonds glinting in the moonlight, tuxedo ties loosened. His brother— the head veterinarian—and his sexy-as-hell lady assistant led the dancing. The redheaded zoologist was just the sort to keep the party going.

Xander's wife, Terri, hadn't been much for dancing, but she'd loved music. When they'd found out she was pregnant, her first reaction was to track down a special device to play classical music for their baby in the womb. Music, she believed, could change a person's life—convey emotions stronger than any other type of language. This belief had also prompted her to find compilations for the animals at the refuge to soothe them. Terri had been his calm and support since they were in first grade, when Xander had been labeled an outcast for already performing three grade levels above the others.

They'd been inseparable since she approached him on the playground that first day and he'd missed her every minute since she'd died.

His daughter—Terri's legacy—meant everything to him.

Washing down the lump in his throat with another swallow of tonic water, he nodded at something or other the politician said about expanding the bird care portion of the refuge's clinic. Xander tucked the info away for later. At least he had the executive power and the portfolio to make that happen, to control something in a world that had denied him control over so damn much.

There was no space tonight for thinking about that now. It wouldn't help the cause his wife had devoted so much time and energy to.

Her volunteer work here had been important to her. When Xander's brother had started at the refuge, Terri's interest ignited. And then she'd discovered her passion, starting foundations to try to channel more funds into reviving the place.

His brother, Easton, oversaw the medical aspect of the refuge as an exotic animal veterinarian with a staff of techs and zoologists. Easton had worked here back in the early days, more concerned with animals than with the money he could make at a bigger, tourist-trap outfit. Xander had supported the refuge's efforts with donations, but now his interest was more personal and yet also more professional. He'd been elected chairman of the board of directors. Terri had wanted him to take that role for years and now she would never know he'd fulfilled her hope that he could grow the refuge.

Damn.

He'd had enough of small talk.

Xander shoved out of his chair. "I appreciate your taking the time to chat and attend. If you'll excuse me, I need to attend to some business, but my brother would thoroughly enjoy talking to you about those clinic additions. I'll get Easton off the dance floor for you."

Making a beeline for his brother who was still dancing with the fire-headed zoologist, Xander shouldered through the partiers, nodding and waving without stopping until he reached the throng of dancers. He tapped Easton on the shoulder.

"Mind if I cut in, brother?"

His eccentric younger brother turned on his heel, his forehead creased, a trickle of sweat beading on his brow. "What's up?"

Easton wore the Prada suit Xander had made sure was delivered for the occasion, but his brother hadn't bothered with a tie. No surprise. Dr. Easton Lourdes had always been more comfortable in khakis and T-shirts.

Xander tipped his head toward the politician still knocking back mixed drinks. "Donor at your nine o'clock. Needs your expertise on possible additions to the aviary in the clinic."

His brother's forehead smoothed and his face folded in a smile, all charm. "Can do." He clapped Xander on the shoulder. "Thanks again for this shindig. It's going to pay off big for the place."

Easton charged past like a man on a mission, leaving his dance partner on the floor alone.

Maureen Burke.

An auburn-haired bombshell, full of brains and energy. She was an Irish native who'd spent much of her life in the States, so her brogue was light. Her degree in zoology along with her rescue experience made her the perfect second-in-command for his brother. Lucky for them she'd received her work visa at exactly the right time. She was extroverted, but also all business. And a woman Xander didn't have to worry was out to take advantage of the Lourdes family fortune passed down for generations. A portfolio Xander had doubled and that women were attracted to when it came to dating Easton.

Maureen was an individual guaranteed not to mistake Easton's attention as interest and an invitation to leave ten voice mails. Maureen was much like Xander when it came to romance.

Not interested.

He'd learned she was divorced and, from her standoffish demeanor just beneath that plush-lipped smile, he got the impression it hadn't been a pleasant split. No doubt the man had been an idiot to let such a gorgeous, intelligent woman walk out of his life.

Xander extended his hand. "Sorry to have stolen your dance partner. I had to send my brother off. Dance with me."

"Dance? With you?" She swept her long red curls back over her shoulder, her face flushed from heat and exertion.

"Is that such a strange request?"

"I didn't expect you to know how to dance, much less to know an Irish jig."

He winced. "An Irish jig?"

She grinned impishly, gesturing to the stage with elegant hands, nails short but painted a glittering gold for the party. "Next up on the band's request list. Your brother double-dog dared me."

Double-dog dare? No wonder Easton had left the dance floor so easily and with a grin on his face. He'd set Xander up.

And Xander wasn't one to back down from a challenge. "I'm a man of many talents. Our mother insisted we boys attend dance classes as teens." He braced his shoulders. "Whatever I don't know, you can teach me."

"Good for your mama."

"And that dance?"

She propped a hand on her hip, her whispery yellow gown hitching along curves as she eyed him with emerald-green eyes. Finally she shrugged. "Sure. Why not? I would like to see the big boss give it a try."

"Remember, you'll have to help me brush up on the steps."

"We'll keep the moves simple." She extended an elbow. "Steel drums playing Irish tunes is a first, not too intricate but still fun."

He bowed before hooking elbows with her. Damn. He'd forgotten how soft a woman's skin felt. Clearing his throat, he mimicked her steps, mixed with a periodic spin. Her hair fanned across his chest as she whipped around.

His body reacted to the simple contact.

Had to be lack of sex messing with his brain.

But holy hell, the dance seemed to go on forever with his blood pressure ramping by the second until, thank God, the band segued to a slower tune. And still he didn't step away. In spite of the twinge of guilt he felt over the surprise attraction, he extended his hands and took her into his arms for a more traditional dance. The scent of citrus—lemons and grapefruit—teased his nose like an aphrodisiac.

Maybe the Irish dance hadn't been such a good idea after all.

He searched for something to say to distract himself from the gentle give of her under his touch, the occasional skim of her body against his. "I'm glad you're enjoying yourself."

"I enjoy anything that makes money for the refuge." Her eyes glimmered in the starlight, loose curls feathering over the top of his hand along her waist. "I love my work here."

"Your devotion is admirable."

"Thank you." Her face flashed with indecision.

"You don't believe me?"

"It's not that. But let's not talk shop right now and spoil the moment. We can talk tomorrow." She chewed her bottom lip. "I have an appointment to see you."

"You do? I don't recall seeing your name on my calendar."

"Not all of us have a personal assistant to keep track of our schedules."

"Am I being insulted?" He had a secretary, but not a personal assistant who followed him around all day like his brother did. Although his brother was known to be an absentminded-professor type.

"No insult meant at all. You've made a great future for yourself and for Rose. It's clear you didn't ride off your family fortune, but increased it. That's commendable." She shook her head, sending her curls prancing along his hand again. "I'm just frustrated. Ignore me. Dance."

Her order came just as the band picked up with a sultry Latin beat.

Maureen Burke danced with abandon.

Throwing herself into this pocket of time, matching the steps of this leanly athletic man with charismatic blue eyes and a sexual intensity as potent as his handsome face.

Brains. Brilliance. A body to die for and a loyal love of family.

Xander Lourdes was a good man.

But not her man.

So Maureen allowed herself to dance with the abandon she never would have dared otherwise. Not now. Not after all she'd been through.

She breathed in the salty air mixed with the scent of fresh burning wood from the bonfire. What a multifaceted word. *Abandon.* She danced with freedom. But she'd also been abandoned and that hadn't felt like freedom at all. The pain. The grief. Being given up on for no good reason other than the fact she wasn't a good fit for her ex-husband's life after all she had put up with. After she'd ignored the urgings of so many friends to leave him and his emotional abuse.

Rejection.

She'd known they had problems. Maureen was always willing to work at broken things. Hell, her never-say-die nature made her compatible and adept in a wildlife refuge. Vows meant something to her. She'd always expected if she ever got divorced it would be because of a major event—physical abuse or drugs. But for nothing more than "I love you but I can't live with you"? Like she'd filled their home with some toxic substance.

More of that negative thinking born of years of his tearing her down until finally—thank God, finally—she'd wised up and realized he was, in fact, the toxin.

So she'd let him go and left their home full of insults and negativity. Hell, she'd left County Cork to get as far away from him and the ache as possible. It wasn't like she had family or anything else holding her back. Her parents were dead and her marriage was a disaster. There'd been nowhere else for her to go except to the US and accept the job in a field of work she loved so much.

She allowed herself to be swept away by the dance, the music and the pulse of the drums pushing through her veins with every heartbeat, faster and faster. Arching timbres of the steel drums urged her to absorb every fiber of this moment.

Too soon, her work visa was due to expire, and officials had thus far denied her requests to extend it. She would have to go home. To face all she'd run from, to leave this amazing place where *abandon* meant beauty and exuberance. Freedom.

The freedom to dance with a handsome man and not to worry that her husband would accuse her of flirting. As if she would run off with any man who looked her way. How long had it taken her to realize his remarks were born of his own insecurities, not her behavior?

She was free to look now, though, at this man with coal-black hair that spiked with the sea breeze and a hint of sweat. His square jaw was peppered with a five-o'clock shadow, his shoulders broad in his tuxedo, broad enough to carry the weight of the world.

Shivering with warm tingles that had nothing to do with any bonfire or humid night, she could feel the attraction radiating off him the same way it heated in her. She'd sensed the draw before but his grief was so well known she hadn't wanted to wade into those complicated waters. But with her return to home looming…

Maureen wasn't interested in a relationship, but maybe if she was leaving she could indulge in—

Suddenly his attention was yanked from her. He reached into his tuxedo pocket and pulled out his cell phone and read the text.

Tension pulsed through his jaw, the once-relaxed, half-cocked smile replaced instantly with a serious expression. "It's the nanny. My daughter's running a fever. I have to go."

And without another word, he was gone and she knew she was gone from his thoughts. That little girl was the world to him. Everyone knew that, as well as how deeply he grieved for his dead wife.

All of which merely made him more attractive.

More dangerous to her peace of mind.

As the morning sun started to spray rays through the night, Xander rubbed the grit from the corners of his eyes, stifling a yawn from the lack of sleep after staying up all night to keep watch over Rose. He'd taken her straight to the emergency room and learned she had an ear infection. Even with the doctor's re-assurance, antibiotics and fever-reducing meds, he couldn't take his eyes off her. Still wearing his tuxedo, he sat in a rocker by her bed. Light brown curls that were slightly sticky with sweat framed her face, her cherubic mouth in a little cupid's bow as she puffed baby breaths. Each rise and fall of her chest reassured him she was okay, a fundamentally healthy sixteen-month-old child who had a basic, treatable ear infection.

A vaporizer pumped moisture into the nursery, which was decorated in white, green and pink, with flowers Terri had called cabbage roses, in honor of their daughter's name. A matching daybed had been included in the room for those nights they just enjoyed watching her breathe. Or for the nanny—Elenora—to rest when needed. A glider was set up in the corner and his mind flooded with memories of Terri nursing their baby in the chair, her face so full of maternal love and hope, all of which had been poured into putting this room together. A week before Rose was born, he and Terri had sat on the daybed, his arms wrapped around her swollen belly, as they'd dreamed of what their child would look like. What she would grow up to accomplish. So many dreams.

Now his brother catnapped in that same space, as he so often did these days, quirky as hell and a never-ending source of support. An image of his brother dancing with Maureen Burke flash through Xander's mind. His brother hadn't had much of a social life lately, either, and even knowing Xander would help Easton if the roles were reversed didn't make it fair to steal so much of his brother's time.

Xander pushed up from the rocker and shook his brother lightly by the shoulder. "Hey, Easton," he said softly. "Wake up, dude. You should head on back to your room."

His brother's eyes blinked open slowly. "Rose?"

"Much better. Her fever's down. I'll still take her to her regular pediatrician for a follow-up, but I think she's going to be fine. She's past needing both of us to keep watch."

"I was sleeping fine, ya know." His lanky brother swung his legs off the bed.

"Folded up like pretzel. Your neck would have been in knots. But thank you. Really. You don't have to stick around. I know you have to work."

"So do you," Easton said pointedly, raking his fingers through his hair.

"She's my kid."

"And you're my brother." His eyes fixed on Xander's. Steady and loyal. They'd always been different but close since their parents traveled the world with little thought of any permanent home or the consistency their kids needed to build friendships. They relied on each other. Even more so after their father died and their mother continued her world traveling ways, always looking for the next adventure in the next country rather than connecting with her children.

And, thank God, Xander's brother could work at any wildlife refuge around the world and he'd chosen to stay on here and help him. That meant the world to him. Easton had done special projects here for Terri, but this place wasn't on the scale of the other places where he could work.

Hell, it wasn't on Xander's scale. But for Terri, for Rose, too, he would put this place on the map. Whatever it took. This was his wife's legacy to their child.

"Thank you."

"No thanks needed other than getting this little

one better." Easton smoothed an affectionate hand over his niece's head. "Well…and a bottle of top-shelf tequila to drink at sunset."

"Put it on the list." A long list, all he owed his brother. But he would find a way to pay him back someday. A kick of guilt pushed him to say, "If you need to move on to a larger job—"

"I wouldn't be needed. Being needed, making a difference—" he shrugged, eyes flicking to Rose "—that's what life's all about."

Xander swallowed hard. Terri had said that to him more than once. God, he missed her. "Fair enough." And before he even realized the thought had crossed his mind, he stopped his brother at the door. "Might you really be sticking around because of a certain red-haired zoologist?"

"Maureen?" Easton said with such incredulity there was no doubting the truthfulness of his state-ment. "No. Absolutely not. There's nothing going on between the two of us. We're too much alike."

Laughing lightly, he shook his head, scratched the back of his neck and chuckled again on his way out the door, leaving Xander more confused than ever. Not because of his brother's denial.

But because of his own relief.

Two

Maureen listened for the familiar *click-click* of her key in her beach cabana door. The double click meant that the teal-colored cabana was, indeed, actually locked. One click meant a well-targeted gust of wind would knock the door in. She would miss these sorts of quirks when she moved out of the brightly painted cabana and tropical Key Largo.

But that wasn't happening yet. Shoving the thought aside, Maureen adjusted her satchel filled with notebooks and began her commute to work. A leisurely five-minute walk.

And today, with the sunshine warming her fair skin, she was content to take in her surroundings as she made her way to the Lourdeses' home residence, built on property they'd bought at the edge of the refuge. Sauntering to the main house—a white beach mansion that always reminded her of the crest of a wave in a storm—she let her mind wander.

Absently, she watched volunteers from town and from farther away gather and disperse on the dock on-site. Even from here, she could hear the bustle of their excitement as the crowd moved toward the fenced and screened areas beneath the white beach mansion on signature Florida Keys stilts.

Eyeing more volunteers who were gathering by the screened areas where recovering animals were kept, she scanned the zone for Easton. Not a trace of him.

Or Xander. After last night, her thoughts tilted back to the dance. To his warm touch, the way he looked after his daughter. The kind of person he was. And those damn blue eyes that cut her to the quick, pierced right through her.

She'd spent most of the night attempting to navigate her sudden attraction to Xander. Not that it really mattered. Instead of admitting that the dance echoed in her dreams last night, she attempted to turn her attention to more practical matters like the school group that was due at the refuge shortly.

Though located on Key Largo, the refuge's secluded location meant tourists didn't wander in haphazardly. The public could access the refuge only through a prearranged guided tour. This policy was one Maureen loved. It made the wildlife refuge into her own kind of sanctuary, one that often felt independent of the tourist traps and straw-hat community of the main part of town. The limited public interaction allowed her to enjoy the mingled scent of salt and animals. There was truly a wildness here that called to some latent part of Maureen's soul.

Surveying her watch, she noted the time. The school children would be here soon. That meant she had to find Easton quickly.

And if she happened to see Xander…well, that'd be just fine by her.

Though, if she were being honest, the thought of accidently on purpose running into him made her giddy. Flashes of last night's dance pulsed in her mind's eye again.

What would she do if she actually ran into him anyway? Running a hand through her ringlet hair, Maureen stifled a sigh as Xander came into view.

Well, she certainly was committed now. At least, committed to some harmless small talk with a man who had pushed her sense of wild abandon into the realm worthy of Irish bards.

Biting the inside of her lip, she dropped her hands to her sides. Xander's smooth walk was uninterrupted as he pulled on his suit coat.

He'd built an office extension onto the refuge when Terri, his wife, had started to volunteer. Terri had fallen in love with Key Largo and her volunteer work. Three years ago, when Maureen had just started with the refuge, Xander had commuted back and forth to Miami for work, using the office at the refuge as a satellite. After Terri passed away, he'd moved here full-time.

Maureen's thoughts lingered for a moment on her memories of Terri. She had been a quiet, gentle woman. It hadn't taken Maureen very long to figure out Terri's heart was bigger than most, and that her kindness and empathy were genuine. Wounded creatures were comforted by Terri's presence. When Terri had become pregnant, she'd begrudgingly performed office work, though Maureen could tell she'd rather have been among the animals.

After she'd passed away, Xander had poured himself into the refuge. In the beginning, Maureen felt like Xander was trying to find some other piece of Terri here.

Now she felt like the refuge had woven its charm for him, too.

Shrugging his suit coat into place, Xander jogged down the long wooden stairway leading from the home on stilts. "Maureen?"

He said it as if he didn't recognize her. But, um, well, maybe she had taken more time with her appearance today. Jeans with a loose-fitting T-shirt was her go-to outfit. Minimal makeup—maybe a wave of a mascara wand over her lashes, a pale lip gloss, her wavy hair confined in a high ponytail. But today she looked considerably...nicer. Her fitted shirt revealed curves, and she'd deepened her lip color, daring a deeper nude that made her seem a bit more put-together, a bit more...well, sultry.

"Of course. Do I look that different?" Maureen's tongue skimmed the back of her teeth, causing her to smile awkwardly, hands flying to a stray strand of her hair that fell in a gentle wave against her chest. So much for nonchalance.

His eyes flicked over her. Slowly—as if he was trying to work something out.

"From last night at the party? Yes."

"We have a group of schoolchildren coming in for a tour this morning," she explained quickly. "They're due any minute and we're shorthanded. Shouldn't you be at work?"

Tilting her head to the side, she squinted at him. His top lip curled up, a smile playing at the corner of his mouth. Raising his eyebrows, he took a step closer, winking at her, more lighthearted than she could remember him being in the past. "Shouldn't you, Maureen?"

The smell of pine drifted into the space between them. Xander's lip was still playfully curled up and she felt a thrill run down her spine as she stared back at him, noticing the way his hair was still damp from a recent shower. Her thoughts stopped there. It felt like ages before she responded.

"I'm looking for your brother." How did Xander manage to keep from perspiring out here in a suit when she already felt like she was melting in a sauna?

Or melting from a different kind of heat.

"Easton's running late. We were both up late last night with Rose."

"You two took care of her?"

"Why is that a surprise?"

"I just assumed someone of your means would lean more on the nanny or call her grandparents."

"My father has passed away and my mother, uh, travels a lot. As for my former in-laws, they can be rather…overpowering. And Elenora needs her rest to be on the top of her game watching Rose while I'm at work. I'm her father. And my brother worried, as well. He also pitched in early this morning when I needed to snag a shower for work. He should be down soon." Xander gestured toward the pathway leading to the offices. "Shall we go?"

She stepped forward, aware of him in step beside her, his shoulder almost brushing hers on the narrow, sandy path. "That's admirable of both of you to take care of Rose. How is she doing?"

"Ear infection, according to the emergency room doctor. I'll be taking her to her pediatrician to follow up today."

"Is there anything I can do to help?" Maureen's thoughts drifted to Rose—the kind of child that adults fawned over. She was sweet, affectionate and filled with life. Maureen had seen testament to that sprinkled all over his office in the form of finger paintings and photographs. A shrine to childhood and a dedicated father.

Maureen's own interaction with Rose always left a smile on her face. With tiny fingers, Rose would reach up to play with Maureen's leather bracelet, touching it carefully as if it was a magical totem. Out of habit, Maureen's own hand flew to her leather bracelet. Feeling the worn leather, she felt assured.

This bracelet had been everywhere with her. A certifying stamp of endurance. "Thanks. But I think we've got it covered. Although I have to admit, it's ironic that it took me and my brother to do one woman's job."

"And somewhere women are sighing."

He laughed.

In the pit of her stomach her nerves became bramble-twisted, much like the palm fronds blowing and tangled by the wind. Those damn blue eyes—they disarmed her senses, unsettling her more than any sounds from wild creatures chattering. Especially today as his gaze darted from her eyes to her lips.

A faint tautness pulled at his cheeks.

Warmth crept up her neck, threatening to flood her cheeks with a schoolgirl blush. *Get it together*, her inner voice scolded. Taking the cue from her sensibility, she drew in a deep breath and straightened her blouse.

"You're needed here to take care of animals." Dropping his gaze, he nodded his head. The momentary flicker of attraction melted off his expression. Xander's tone and eyes returned to their normal bulldog, businessman-slate stare.

"Of course. She's your child and doesn't really know me well." She held up her hands. "I've overstepped and I apologize."

He sighed. "I apologize. You're being helpful and I'm being an ass. I have a reputation for that."

She stayed silent.

"Not going to deny it?" His lip twitched upward.

"I wouldn't dare call the big boss anything so insulting."

He laughed. Hard. "You are surprising me left and right. Not at all how I've perceived you in the past."

"You thought about me?" Words tumbled out of her mouth before she thought better of them.

"As your employer."

"That makes things tricky. And you've had…a difficult year."

"Fourteen months. It's been fourteen months and three days." His voice lost an octave, felt like a whisper on a breeze.

"I'm so very sorry for your loss." An ache of deep empathy pushed hard against her chest. She'd seen the love Xander and Terri had for each other, a love she'd hoped to have in her own marriage.

"Me, too." His eyes met hers as a gust of island breeze carried the scent of flowers and the sound of distant motors. "Rose means everything to me. She's all I have left of Terri. I would do anything for my daughter but sometimes—" he thrust a hand through his tousled hair, his head tipping back as he looked up toward the sky "—I just feel like I'm short-changing her."

She touched his arm lightly. "You're tired, like any parent. And you're an amazing father, here for her, along with your brother. And Rose truly has a wonderful nanny. Elenora genuinely cares about her."

"Of course she does. I can see the affection they share." Was this the kind of thing she was supposed to say to a man baring his heart and acknowledging his pain? Maureen found the familiar spot in her bottom lip and chewed, wishing she could say something—anything—to take the hurt out of his voice.

"I spend time with her every day."

"I know that, too." She hadn't realized how much she'd noticed about his routine before. "You don't have to explain yourself to me. It's clear you love her."

"I do. She's everything to me."

"She's a lucky little girl."

The space between them thinned and now, shoulder to shoulder, she noticed how the pine soap pushed against a symphony of coffee beans and mint.

Turning to face her, his blue eyes sparked. He took half a step toward her, his own lips parted slightly as he searched her expression.

She stopped chewing her lip and tilted her head to the side to stare back at him, stomach fluttering the longer his gaze held hers.

"Thank you for your help last night organizing the gala."

"Thank you for the dance last night."

They stayed like that for a few moments until the buses were pulling up and pulling them back into reality. Away from whatever had electrified the air between them.

A full day in the office left Xander desperate for some salt air and sunshine. He'd worked, taken Rose to the pediatrician and had just settled her down for a nap. He'd read her a story before she drifted off to sleep. With the nanny on-call, he'd decided to take his brother up on his invitation to check the water samples from the nearby swamp.

He tried to convince himself he was only going out on the boat to become better acquainted with the procedures so he'd be of more use at the next fundraiser. The fact that Maureen also was on the boat was pure coincidence. Xander tried to tell himself that was an accurate representation of reality.

His attempt to delude himself, however, was a hard sell, it turned out. He couldn't deny he wanted to be there. He'd looked forward to seeing Maureen and finding out if this attraction to her was just an anomaly.

Easton, his assistant, Portia, Maureen and Xander were all in swimsuits as the low-slung boat putted its way through the water. He tried not to notice Maureen's toned legs and the way her lavender one-piece swimsuit hugged her curves. Even her messy windwhipped ponytail was sexy as hell.

Maureen was also a stark contrast to Portia Soto, his brother's assistant. Portia was also in a one-piece bathing suit, but a long patterned sarong swaddled her body. Portia embodied prim and proper. No detail was too minute to escape her notice. Portia adjusted her oversize hat and sunglasses, though she looked anxious.

So far, Xander couldn't understand why Portia had taken the job as his brother's assistant. She was efficient and talented. Of that, there was no doubt. But she seemed to be timid the majority of the time, not necessarily the sort that came immediately to mind when thinking of staff for a wild animal refuge.

Easton sat beside his assistant, who'd plastered herself in the seat with her back pressed against it, her fingers gripping the edge. Poor thing. She looked absolutely miserable and terrified. And while Xander's first instinct was to talk to the trembling woman, he couldn't help how his eyes seemed to always find their way back to Maureen.

"Would you like to return to the shore? You don't have to come with us every time," Maureen said gently, touching Portia's arm.

"The doctor relies on my notes." She nodded to the bag in her hand, though Portia's eyes darted nervously to the brackish water and swamp animals outside. Clearly this job pushed her limits and yet here she was, anyway.

"They are helpful," he said absently while leaning over the edge. Wind tore through the boat, pressing Easton's blue swim trunks and white T-shirt hard against his body.

Maureen clucked her tongue. "A gator's going to bite your arm off one day."

Portia turned green.

Maureen's brogue lilted like the waves. "I'm only teasing."

Portia looked down and eased one hand free to pull her recorder from her waterproof bag. She began mumbling notes into the mike.

Maureen angled down to Easton. "I think she's plotting your demise."

"Possibly. But we have an understanding. We both need each other."

"It just seems strange she would take a job that scares her silly."

"I pay well. Not many enjoy this. I trust her and that counts for a helluva lot. Besides, I'm convinced she has an adventurous spirit buried underneath all that starch." His grin was wicked as he turned to face Maureen. That was his brother all right—always pushing people's comfort levels and making them laugh.

"If she doesn't have a heart attack first."

Portia chimed in, hands once again finding the edge of the seat cushions for stability. "Or die from some flesh-eating bacteria."

Easton laughed, his chuckles echoing over the water before he returned to his work again.

Xander caught his brother's eye before Easton turned to face Maureen. Something sly passed over Easton's expression and he quickly raised his brow to Xander before fully focusing on Maureen. "I'm damn sorry you're going to be leaving us."

"Me, too. This is a dream job." Her lithe arm extended out to the impossible shade of green water that surrounded them. Her attention seemed fixed on an imaginary spot on the horizon and Xander followed her gaze, trying to imagine what she was thinking about. Did she want to go home? It certainly didn't seem so from her crestfallen face, and she had asked him to look into extending the visa to complete her work here. He hadn't heard back, but then, that news would have gone to her and apparently the answer hadn't been positive.

Still, her face showed such distress, Xander couldn't help but wonder if it was about more than work.

Easton let out a low whistle. "And you're sure there's no way to extend the work visa?"

"It's been denied. Your brother even had the company lawyers review my paperwork to help, but with things tightening down regarding immigration, my request has been denied…" Maureen glanced back at Xander, her eyes as green as the crystal waters.

Did she know he could hear them?

He did his best to seem disinterested and aloof, channeling years of cutthroat business meetings to school his features into a mask of neutrality.

Easton's eyes momentarily flicked back to Xander. For a brief moment he swore Easton's head nodded slightly. Was that a sign to pay attention? What did his brother have planned?

"Xander has a lot of his time and energy—and heart—invested in this place."

"That, he does. I was surprised to see him dance last night."

"Who would have thought he could dance a jig?" Easton winked over his shoulder at his brother, making it clear he knew full well his brother could hear every word. "Who would have thought he would dance at all? That has certainly been in question since Terri died."

"She was a lovely lady." Maureen's voice meshed into the sounds of the nearby birds.

Xander tried not to look desperate as he strained to hear the rest of the conversation.

"She was. We all miss her. Her parents do, too, obviously. We always will. But I can't help hoping my brother will find a way to move on." Easton's lips had thinned into a smile and he stuck her with a knowing glance.

Maureen shook her head and tendrils of red hair fell out of her loose ponytail. "You're reading too much into a dance."

"I didn't say a thing. You did." A taunting, brotherly tone entered Easton's voice. He lifted up his hands to her, palms out in an exaggeration of placation.

"I'm definitely not making a move on your brother." The words were jagged on her tongue. Even from his seat, Xander could see pain jutting into Maureen's normally fair, bubbly features.

"Again, I didn't say that. You did."

"I'm divorced."

"I know."

Shrugging her shoulder, she leaned against the rail of the boat. "It was ugly."

"So very sorry to hear that."

"The past is past. I'm focused on my present and my job."

"Is that the reason you're so determined to stay here? Because your ex is back home?" Easton's eyes flicked back to Xander who pretended not to notice. But the truth was that his heart pulsated in his chest as he continued to listen to their conversation. A bad divorce? He couldn't help but wonder what had happened.

"Staying here is certainly easier. Fresh starts often are."

"It's not over yet."

"I appreciate your optimism."

"Um, hello?" Portia's voice rang out, urgency coloring every syllable. "Um, Doctor?"

"Yes, Ms. Soto?" Easton turned to face her.

"I'm getting seasick." And with that, Portia pulled herself up to the railing, turned a particularly sunset shade of scarlet and hurled the contents of her stomach overboard.

Xander reacted, setting their course back to the dock. Portia needed land, and fast.

They weren't too far away. Within minutes the dock was in sight.

And so were Xander's in-laws. It was never a good sign when they showed up from Miami unannounced. A pit knotted in his stomach and he felt his jaw tighten and clench.

Xander leaped off the boat as soon as it stabilized and helped Portia out. She'd gone ghost-pale and her hands were clammy—clearly she was much more seasick than she'd let on. Once Portia's feet were on solid ground, she covered her mouth, nodded politely at Xander's in-laws and dashed up to the house, probably stifling the urge to hurl the whole way.

His in-laws surveyed the landscape with eyes that

revealed complete disgust. His mother-in-law's gaze followed Portia up the slope to the house. Delilah's brow arched, a silent conversation seemed to unfold between her and Jake, Xander's father-in-law.

So the verdict was out on this place. They'd hated it and did little to try to disguise that.

Jake looked at Portia's disappearing form and then back at Xander. Disapproval danced in his gaze.

Xander stifled the urge to grind his teeth. Did they actually think he was interested in Portia? And was that really any of their business to pass judgment on his dating life? Of course they all missed Terri, but she was gone, for over a year, and that was the tragic reality.

Besides, he wanted to tell them they had it all wrong, anyway. Portia wasn't his type. Xander didn't know why they'd assumed she'd be the kind of woman he was interested in, and he didn't want them to believe he hadn't loved their daughter with his whole soul. Xander certainly didn't want them to think she'd been so easily replaced.

The protest nearly formed against his tongue when reality jabbed him. Portia was polished, quiet, reserved… As far as types went, she shared a lot of Terri's qualities.

But Portia had never crossed his mind. Not once. Not in passing. There was no draw to her. Not like there was to the fiery Maureen. Xander's eyes flicked quickly to Maureen. She was helping Easton dock the boat.

Turning his attention back to his in-laws, he surveyed them, trying to anticipate the reason for this unannounced visit.

Jake and Delilah Goodwin were good people, if intrusive. They were what the news media deemed helicopter parents.

Xander had always imagined their hovering had everything to do with the circumstances of Terri's birth. For years Delilah and Jake had tried to conceive but never could. The doctors had told them it was practically impossible for them to become pregnant. But somehow Delilah had been able to conceive and carry Terri to full term. The miracle child. Their only child.

Terri had been pampered and sheltered her whole life. They'd treated Terri like spun glass, like a fragile thing that needed protection from everything and everyone. Now having a daughter of his own, he understood the motivation and desire, but Jake and Delilah had taken hovering to its extreme.

Xander watched as Jake gave Delilah's hand a quick squeeze. His business instincts told him the gesture was one of support. He understood that. Terri's death had changed everything.

Delilah straightened her heirloom pearls on her neck, the only piece of jewelry that spoke to their enormous wealth. They were kind people, but they were used to dictating orders. They weren't the compromising type.

"We heard our grandchild is ill and you're out here. Who's watching her?" Jack said, his voice even but stern.

"She's napping while Elenora watches over her. Rose has an ear infection. We went to the emergency room last night and the pediatrician today."

Laying a manicured hand to her chest, Delilah stiffened. "She could have a relative watching her."

"She does. Her father and her uncle." Xander kept his tone neutral, doing his best to remember that they didn't mean to be insulting or accusatory.

"Both of whom are out partying on a boat," Delilah continued, her voice shrill and unforgiving.

The correction was gentle but necessary. He wished Terri was here to help him navigate this. "Working."

"Okay, then. Working. She could have her grandmother all day."

"I'm appreciative of your offer to help. Who told you about the ear infection?"

Delilah waved her hand dismissively. "Someone on the staff when I phoned to say hello."

To check up, more likely. His in-laws made no secret of the fact that they wanted custody of Rose. He would feel a lot more comfortable welcoming them for visits if they weren't taking notes and plotting the whole damn time.

He ground his teeth and tried to be as reasonable as possible. He didn't want to upset his daughter's world by having her taken from her own father. "Rose will be awake in about an hour. If you would like to stay for lunch, you can play with her when she wakes."

He glanced over his shoulder, checking on his

brother and Maureen. Easton was tying the boat off along the dock while Maureen gathered up the samples. But that wasn't what caught Xander's eye. A massive gator swam in the dock area and bumped into the boat. The low-slung boat was tipped off balance and his eyes darted to Maureen, who was leaning over the railing.

Three

Water swirled around Maureen as she plummeted into the murky bay off the side of the boat.

Swimming had never been an issue for her. In Ireland, her childhood adventures had often unfolded in rivers and lakes. The water called to her. When she was young, she'd hold her breath and dive in undaunted. She'd even told her parents she was searching for kelpie—mythical Irish water horses. They were dangerous creatures of legend—sometimes drowning mortals for sport. At eight, Maureen was convinced that she could find kelpie and clear up the misconception. Her inclination to help and heal ran deep, to her core.

But here, in the swampy waters of Key Largo, there was no mythical creature that might whisk her to the bottom and drown her. No, in this water, an alligator slinked by. An animal that actually had the capacity to knock life from her lungs.

She tread water, schooling her breathing into calm inhales and exhales. Or at least, this was the attempt she was making. Boggy, slimy weeds locked around her ankle, twisting her into underwater shackles.

Adrenaline pushed into her veins, her heart palpitating as she tried to force a degree of rigidity into her so-far-erratic movements.

From her memory depths, she recalled a time not unlike this one. She'd been swimming in Lake Michigan after her parents had relocated to Michigan. She'd been caught in weeds then, too, but her father had been there to untangle her. And that lake had lacked primitive dinosaur-like predators, which had made the Lake Michigan moment decidedly less dramatic.

Eyes flashing upward, she caught the panic flooding Xander's face.

Ready to help her.

The weeds encircling her ankle pulled against her. *Damn*. How'd she managed to become so ensnared so quickly? The pulse of the tide slashed into her ears, pushing her against the boat.

A loss of control kicked into her stomach. She heard vague shouting. Easton? Maybe. His voice seemed far away.

The grip on her ankle pulled taut, forcing her below the surface. The more she tried to tread water, to grab hold of the boat, the more she was pulled down. A new sort of tightness tap-danced on her chest. A mouthful of salt water belabored her breathing.

A vague sense of sound broke through her disorientation. Xander's voice. That steadying baritone. "Maureen, I'm coming!"

Words drifted to her like stray pieces of wood. Her salt-stung vision revealed Xander's muscled form coming toward her. She made out the people behind him—his in-laws. Even from here, blurry vision and all, she read the concern in their clasped forms.

In an instant Xander was there, face contorted in worry. With an arm, he stabilized her against the boat. Air flooded her lungs again.

"I'm okay. I can swim. I just need to get my foot untangled from the undergrowth."

"Roger." He started to dive.

She grasped his arm. "Be careful of the—"

His gaze moved off to the side where the gator lingered with scaly skin and beady eyes. "I see. And the sooner we get out of here the better."

He disappeared underwater, a trail of small bubbles the only trace of him. Sinking fear rendered a palatable thrum in her chest—a war drum of anxiety. The gator disappeared under water.

Time stood on a knife-edge.

Suddenly she felt a palm wrap around her ankle and release her from the weeds. On instinct, she drew her knee to chest.

Xander followed. The edge of worry ebbed but refused to fade.

"I'm sure you can swim. But humor me. You may not know you're injured."

"I don't want to slow you—"

"And I don't want to hang out here in the swamp with gators and God only knows what else in addition to the leaking gas. Quit arguing." No room for negotiation in that tone. It must be the same voice Xander used in boardroom meetings.

"Okay, then. Swim."

His arms around her, she felt warmth leap from his body to hers. Feeling small and protected for the first time in ages. The muscles in his arm grew taught and retracted as he moved them through the water. Steadying her breathing, pushing her fear far away.

The water gave way to mucky sand and he helped her wade through that all the way to the shoreline.

Her body shook of its own accord. As if by reflex, he wrapped her into a tight hug and her head fit snugly beneath his chin.

The world, which a moment ago was filled with panic and fear, stilled. His breath on her cheek warmed her bones with more intensity than the tropical sun.

In that space, adrenaline fell back into her bloodstream. But fear didn't motivate that move this time. Awareness did as he held her close, breathing faster, somehow keeping time with her ragged heart. His body felt like steel against hers as she pulled away from him, her eyes catching his, watching as they fell away to her lips.

She hadn't imagined it, then, noting his desire.

"Maureen?" Her name sent the world crashing back into place. Willing her eyes away from his, she looked over her shoulder to see his in-laws and Easton standing a short distance away.

Knowing he needed coverage, even if just for a moment, she turned to face them, careful to stay angled in front of Xander. As if he'd done it a thousand times before, his hands fell to her shoulders. A mild but welcome distraction.

Xander's in-laws were visibly distraught.

"Are you okay?" Xander's father-in-law asked, face crumpled like he smelled something rotting. Maureen nodded dully, afraid her words might betray something private and real about this moment.

The man shifted focus from Maureen to Xander. "And you?"

"Yes. Thankfully. More of a scare than any real harm." His hands squeezed Maureen's shoulder blades before dropping. Immediately she felt the echo of his absence from her skin.

His mother-in-law sniffed in response. "Honestly. What if that had been Rose? I'm just glad she wasn't out here. A nature refuge is lovely, of course—" ice entered her words "—but such a dangerous, unpredictable place isn't so well suited for *our* grandchild."

Maureen squinted at the woman's response, which felt more like a warning than anything else.

Hours separated him from the gator run-in and he still couldn't think straight.

He'd always been a pro at compartmentalizing events, locking his personal life away so he could focus on whatever task at hand. That proved infinitely difficult with this afternoon's events.

As if his mind was a film loop, he kept revisiting Maureen falling in the water, a gator just a few feet away. The moment she looked like she was struggling sent him tumbling into action—a reflex and urge so primal, he couldn't ignore it.

Nor could he ignore the way she'd looked, soaked to the bone in her swimsuit. The feel of her shuddering with relief when they were on solid ground. How that relief reverberated in his own gut as he'd looked at her full lips.

There was no denying how turned on he was. The connection he'd felt to her in that beachside embrace had made him so damn aware of her. Sure, she'd always been attractive. He knew that, but there was something so sexy about the way she'd endured the gator run-in.

He wanted her, down to his core. All day, his thoughts drifted to her.

Did life ever get easy?

Watching his in-laws with his daughter provided a quick answer to that question. Delilah and Jake weren't mean—they were matter-of-fact. Particular. Things had to be just so.

Reflecting back on Terri's perfect makeup and clothes, he saw what a lifetime of being scrutinized could do. How that constant second-guessing had sometimes wrought Terri up with anxiety. Especially when her parents came for a visit. She'd agonize on the arrangement of pillows and the tenderness of the pasta. Her mother and father always had a critique, a method of alleged perfection. Deep down, he knew they meant well.

Seeing Delilah straighten Rose's bow and quietly comment on staying proper rubbed him the wrong way. He wanted his daughter to grow up confident in her own worth.

He wanted to bring up his child.

"You know, Xander, we could help you with Rose. Keep her until school starts. We're retired now and we can devote all of our attention to her." Delilah's polished voice trilled. She had been hunched over Rose, examining the little girl's drawing.

"Ah, well, I know she looks forward to seeing you both. I think that helps enough," he said sympathetically. The pain of loss seemed to form a permanent line on her brow.

"Barry, our family friend and lawyer, you remember him? He mentioned that the court might see an arrangement with us to suit Rose better. We know how hard you work. We have the time to devote to her that you may not right now." Jake stood behind Xander, resting a hand on his shoulder.

The blood beneath his skin fumed, turned molten. He had to keep his cool. "Well, I know how much you love Rose. But it's time for her to nap. She's still not feeling well."

Smoothing her dress, Delilah nodded. "Yes, she does need rest."

"I'm sure you feel similarly. You both should probably get settled in your hotel." His even tone held a challenge in it. He needed separation from them. Boundaries.

Especially now, because their intent had come into full view. They were here to spy on his proficiency as a father.

A more sinister thought entered his mind. What if they just snatched her away? It echoed in his mind as he saw them off the property and as he walked back into the room where his daughter slept. He looked at Elenora, a woman in her fifties with kind brown eyes, and left instructions with a caution about the issue with his in-laws. Elenora had to stay with Rose, and if anyone tried to come on the property, he was to be alerted at once.

The woman nodded her understanding. Feeling satisfied, he walked to his other unofficial charge. He went to find Maureen. Needed to make sure she was okay after her accident. There had been no time to actually check on her—not with his in-laws so close by.

Striding over to the clinic—another retrofitted and well-windowed building—his pace quickened. An urgency to move filled him. The stress of his in-laws, their constant reminders of the danger of the refuge and the way he was raising Rose. It all slammed into him.

Opening the door to the clinic, the sour smell of oil assaulted him. He turned the first corner in the building to see Maureen and a gaggle of oil-soaked seabirds. When the boat tipped, oil had seeped into the water and drenched the feathers of about five birds. The refuge had rounded them up for cleaning.

Maureen worked quickly, using the Dawn dish soap generously to lift the layers of oil from delicate feathers. He studied her, once again reminded of the intense gut-kick he'd felt earlier when she'd fallen into the water. The fear of loss knotted. He hated that fear.

Maureen cooed at the birds, mimicking their squawks with absolute precision. From a distance, and if he didn't know any better, he'd felt like she was actually talking to them. A real conversation. Her heart seemed to soar with delight as every inky layer of oil was lifted from the feathers of the bird.

Easton, a few feet away in the exam room, diligently looked over every bird Maureen had expertly cleaned.

Her hair was wet and piled on top of her head in a loose topknot with a few spiral curls escaping. She wore surgical scrubs. Apparently she'd only taken a quick shower to remove the muck from herself before going to work again.

She probably hadn't even thought about getting her own ankle examined. So like Maureen. So tender.

As she stood rinsing a bird, a smile on her lips, he felt the world slip away again. Mesmerized by her grace and movements.

And so kind. That fact, her empathy and patience,

it was the remedy he needed. One that might even strike favor with his hard-to-please in-laws.

Gently, Maureen worked the oil out of the bird's left wing feathers, careful not to squeeze too tightly and damage the delicate bones. Moments had fallen away before she registered someone lingering by the door frame.

Not just someone. Xander.

Heat flooded into her cheeks as she remembered the way their bodies had pressed up against each other after the gator run-in.

"Are you okay? That was quite a spill you took."

She shrugged her shoulders, tongue unable to articulate any of her whirring thoughts.

"What makes a girl—hell, anyone—want to wrestle with alligators?" He inched closer.

"They don't bite nearly as hard as the ones in the boardroom," she volleyed back, thankful to find her voice again. He unnerved her fully.

"Funny." A puff of a laugh teased against his teeth, leaving behind a serpentine hiss.

"And I can outrun them."

"Also funny. But seriously, why this career?"

A loaded question. Freedom. This career awarded her a sense of sky and life the way nothing else could. "Why any career? Why would you want to stay inside all the time?"

"I enjoy the corporate challenge and I have a head for business. Without that, places like this would close down. It almost did." A defensive edge filled his tone.

She flashed a toothy smile, raising an eyebrow as a soap bubble floated in the space between them. "True enough. And without me, places like this wouldn't exist. I wanted to be a veterinarian. I just had to find my niche."

"So someone threw an alligator in your pool and you knew?" His lips parted into an incredulous smile and she found it hard to concentrate. Averting her gaze, she turned back to the double-crested cormorant, the bird made its traditional guttural noise that sounded much like a grunting pig. Funny. Endearing. It helped her re-center, refocus on her work with the greenish-black bird that sported an adorable orange neck.

"I was actually out on a field trip for school. My work group got separated from the rest and we were lost, wandering around deeper into the moors. The fog rolled in and we couldn't see what was around our feet. It freaked out the others in the group, but I found that soup of nature…fascinating. I just wanted to reach down in there and run my fingers through the mist. I felt…connected. I knew." She gestured to the world around her. "This is what I'm supposed to do with my life."

"You are…an incredible woman."

She felt the blush heat her cheeks. His compliment shouldn't matter but it did. Her self-esteem had taken some serious dings during her marriage. "Thank you. I'm just a lucky one."

"Hard work certainly increases the odds of good luck."

"Still, life isn't always evenhanded." In fact, she felt like it was often like an out-of-balance scale. All the counterweights were askew. Looking at him now, leaning casually against the workstation, definitely riled her sense of evenhandedness. Being attracted to him was not without complications. Serious work-altering complications. And then, there was the problem of her work visa expiring.

His face went somber. "True enough."

"Oh, God." She touched his arm. "I'm sorry. I didn't mean to be insensitive."

"It's okay. Really. I can't spend the rest of my life having people measure their every word around me. I wouldn't want that for Rose, either. I want her to grow up in a world of happiness."

Searching for some level ground, she offered, "I'm sure she's being pampered to pieces by her grand-parents."

His face went even darker.

"What did I say wrong?" Her stomach knotted.

"It's not you. It's just that my relationship with them has become strained since Terri died. They miss her, I understand that. We're all hurt."

"Everyone could tell how much you loved each other."

"We'd known each other all our lives." His voice was filled with a hollow kind of sadness.

"So you've known her parents as long, too. They should be like parents to you, as well."

He barked out a laugh. "If only it was that simple."

"I don't want to pry."

He shook his head. "You're not. They blame me for not taking care of her. I was working late when she died. If I'd been home on time, maybe I would have seen the symptoms, gotten her to the hospital in time…"

In his tone, she could hear how many times he'd replayed that night in his head. Played the what-if game. She knew how painful the potential of what-if could be.

"You can't blame yourself." Her voice was gentle but firm.

"I do. They do." Quieter still, he took a step forward, buried his face in his hands as if to shut out any chance of redemption. But Maureen knew a thing or two about "phoenixing"—the importance of being birthed by fire and ash.

"Easton told me the doctors said there was nothing that could have been done."

She reached a soapy hand for his, certain Xander needed a small show of comfort. Her heart demanded that of her.

"I wish I could believe that. I wish we all could."

"That has to have left a big hole in your life."

"It has."

"I'm so sorry." And she was. So damn sorry for how things had played out for him. For the burden of a future he'd glimpsed but could never have. She understood that sort of pain.

"I have our child. And I can't change things."

"Stoic."

He leveled a sardonic look her way. "The problem with that?"

"Nothing."

"Even I know that when a woman says nothing, she means something." He half grinned, an attempt at light in a shadowed spot. A good sign. A necessary one. And Maureen used that light to ask the question that had burned a hole in her mind all day.

"I just wonder who…"

"Who what?"

"Who helped you through that time?" Immediately she regretted the push for information. Stammering, she continued. "Th-that's too personal. Forget I said anything."

He waved his hand, dismissing her retraction. "Holding my daughter comforted me. There's no way to make the pain go away. Enough talk about me. What about you? Tell me your life history if you expect mine."

"I'm from Ireland." An evident truth and perhaps a cop-out answer meant to delay going deeper.

"Great mystery there, lass." He re-created a thick brogue, sounding like an Irishman in a BBC production. The gesture tugged a smile at the corners of her mouth.

"My accent's not that thick."

"True. And why is that?"

She looked up at him through her lashes as she finished the last bird's wing. "My father worked for an American-based company in Michigan for ten years."

"Is that what drew you back here?"

"Maybe. I needed a change after my divorce and this opening came up. I got the work visa. Here I am." That was the heart of the story. No lies, but nothing to sink his teeth into. Maureen was always much more comfortable asking people how they felt and what they needed than sharing her own details, especially after her divorce.

"And now it's time to go home." He tipped his head to the side. "You don't seem pleased about that. I imagine your family has missed you."

"They weren't pleased with me for splitting with my ex. They accused me of choosing my job over my marriage."

"Your husband wasn't interested in coming with you?"

"No, he wasn't. I didn't ask, actually. We'd already split by then, but my parents didn't know." She shook her head. "But I don't want to talk about that. Nothing more boring than raking over the coals of a very cold divorce." The need to change the subject ached in her very bones.

"Whatever you wish."

Time to shift back to Xander. To something of the present. "What brought you out here?"

"I need your help."

"Is there an animal loose?"

He held a hand to his chest, acting as if he'd been wounded by her insinuation. "I think you just insulted my manhood. I may not be my brother, but I can handle a stray critter."

Damn, he was too handsome and charming for his own good—or her sanity.

She considered his words for a moment before pressing further. "Snakes?"

"Sure." He nodded.

"Birds?"

"A net and gentle finesse?"

"A key deer?"

"I could chase it with the four-wheeler."

The image of Xander loaded up in a four-wheeler corralling key deer sent her giggling. She'd never seen this fun side of him before and she couldn't help but be enchanted by the flirtatious game. After all, it was safe, not likely to lead anywhere. "Gators?"

"Stay away from the gators."

She rolled her eyes. "Whatever. Quite frankly, I would rather handle the gator than wrestle the numbers and executives you deal with." She shuddered. "And living in an office? No, thank you."

"But you'll stay in the boat when it comes to the alligators from now on."

"Of course." She winked playfully at him, enjoying the lighthearted, no-pressure moment. "What did you want to ask me?"

"How's your work visa extension progressing?"

Ugh. Now that was a sobering turn to the conversation. This wasn't new information. The question confused her. "Not well."

"I can help you."

"You'll put in a good word for me?"

"I already did that and clearly that's not enough."

"Then what are you proposing?"

"That's just it. I'm proposing."

His words thundered in her brain, a reality she couldn't quite locate yet.

Proposing?

Four

The words hung heavy in the air between them. She blinked at him. Not a good sign.

Her head bobbed side to side, as if she was replaying his words. He watched as her practiced hands put the now-clean bird in a cage, the greenish hues of the feathers more vibrant, the orange neck glowing again. Astonishment pulled at her lips while the bird perched and gave its little grunting honk of joy. Maureen, however, stayed silent.

There was no enthusiastic agreement coming. He could see that now.

But that only made him all the more determined that this was the right path for both of them.

Maureen frantically scanned the room. Looking for Easton and the other technicians, no doubt, her eyes wide as she turned back to him. "Proposing what, exactly? A proposition?"

"Not propositioning you. Proposing *to* you."

"Pro…posing?" she stuttered in a shrill whisper. "To me? As in 'get married' proposing? You and I?"

"Pro-pose! Pro-pose!" screeched a three-foot-high parrot named Randy who kept watch over this workstation when he wasn't in the aviary. The parrot marched around a perch near the window, his presence somehow calming the traumatized new birds.

"A marriage of convenience. So yes, proposing we get married." This was a practical arrangement. A business deal that would suit them both. And damn lucky for them, they had the spark and heat that could make a marriage more than just a contract arrangement.

"So the work visa is no longer an issue and I could stay in the States?" Her teeth skimmed her bottom lip. He could see the reality of his offer taking root in her.

"And my in-laws won't stand a chance at taking my daughter."

Her brow furrowed. "You want a mother for your daughter? Is that fair to her to have her think of me that way and then I leave?"

"She has a mother and her mother is dead. I'm not asking you to replace her, not by a long shot. My daughter has a father who loves her more than anything on this earth and she has the best nanny money can hire in Elenora."

Maureen's shoulders relaxed down at least a little. "What exactly are you asking of me then?"

"I need my in-laws to quit threatening me. And I do know you will be a positive influence in Rose's life while you're here. I'm damn good at interviewing. I don't expect you to spend time with her if that's not what you want." He just needed a convincing façade to show the world. The appearance of cohesion. Unity. The sort of thing that would even appease Delilah. She could take this information back to their family lawyer. It'd be a helluva lot tougher for his in-laws to gain custody of Rose if a nuclear family manifested.

"Of course I would—"

Shaking his head, he leaned forward on the sink's countertop. "My mother-in-law—hell, everyone—will sense it if you're faking the emotion. It should be genuine."

"Won't she wonder why we married so quickly?"

"Let her wonder. This is a temporary arrangement. By the time your work situation is settled and my court battle is solid, then we can split. Rose'll be too young to understand. And I trust you to be kind."

She touched her forehead. "I need time to think about this. It's just so…calculated."

Xander made his fortune through careful calculations. He knew how to weigh options, to choose the most sensible path for the biggest gains. He had a knack for this sort of interaction. He couldn't help it if it appeared calculated. It was his skill set.

"You don't have the luxury of time and neither do

I, so think fast. Our futures—Rose's future—depend on your decision."

All of his years in boardroom coups and takeovers had taught him two things: when someone would cave and when someone wouldn't. Examining her lip-chewing and her continuously wringing hands, he could see Maureen's resolve crumbling. Not only for her future—he knew how much she wanted to stay in the States—but also for Rose. For the child who needed to be protected. Xander knew Maureen couldn't turn her back on any living being in need. Especially not a vulnerable little girl.

Damned if that didn't make Maureen all the more appealing to him—and perhaps a bit riskier than he'd anticipated.

Xander took his seat at the head of the dining room table. Dinner with his in-laws. An informal affair, as always, since he opened up his dining room to anyone still on the grounds volunteering. It wasn't unusual for people to come and go, filling a plate of food and joining the family or making their own little groupings out on the patio area. The cost of the food was nothing to him compared to the compassionate volunteer help of the people who helped fulfill Terri's mission here.

And he appreciated the love and attention they showered on Rose. She had quite an extended family, not blood-related but connected by affection.

He was doing his best to build a life for her here and he hoped like hell his former in-laws could recognize the depth and thought he put into parenting. He did not take this responsibility lightly. Neither did his brother.

And now that Maureen had agreed—albeit reluctantly—to his proposal, all would see he had a stable environment in place here for Rose. In fact, he'd asked Maureen to bring Rose in after the little one woke from her nap to help set the stage of their connection.

The three of them.

Xander had to keep his cool and not let the threat of a custody battle cloud their visit. Even Easton was keeping his normally outrageous personality in check, seated at the other end of the table.

Xander lifted the wine carafe. "I trust your hotel suite is comfortable?"

He poured Delilah a glass of wine. Her manicured fingers touched the base of the wine stem, gray eyes steadily focused on the merlot cascading from bottle to glass.

Jake answered, "Of course. It's a beautiful hotel. Big bay windows. Polite bellman."

He cast a look at his wife. The nod she gave back was practically imperceptible, but the subtle gesture didn't escape Xander's notice.

"You know, Xander, we love Rose. We see so much of Terri in her."

Xander stopped pouring the wine. "I know. I see that, too."

"Where is she, Xander? Our visit was too short today," Delilah pressed.

"She's sleep—" His voice trailed off as Maureen entered the dining room. With Rose. "—ing."

His in-laws followed his gaze, resting on Maureen and the child. *His* child, who looked so damn comfortable in her arms. Rose's face had regained color and her eyes, finally cleared of their earlier drowsiness, sparkled with interest. Rose giggled and blew baby kisses at her uncle Easton, who winked back.

After examining the sweet expression of ease on his daughter's face, Xander's gaze drank in the curves exposed by Maureen's lilac-colored sundress. Heart hammering, he swallowed. Hard.

Delilah practically leaped out of her chair, pushing to see her grandchild.

"I'll take her off your hands. It's late and Xander shouldn't keep you here after hours."

"Actually, I'm here for dinner." If she noticed Delilah's disappointment as the woman slid back into her chair, Maureen didn't let on.

Brow furrowing, he tried to read Maureen's expression for a hint of what she was thinking. And quickly, before his in-laws read the silent exchange between them. But he wasn't going to argue. In fact, he had to admit to being charged by the way she kept him on his toes. "Yes, I'll take Rose while you help yourself to dinner." He gestured to the sideboard with the plates and supper buffet, china serving platters laden with crab-covered snapper, coconut shrimp, asparagus and diced red potatoes. Small baskets of fluffy biscuits and hushpuppies rested at the end of the line of steaming offerings.

Maureen shook her head. "It's okay. I'll hold her until one of you finishes your food. I've missed her today." With admirable dexterity, she held Rose on one hip while putting together a dessert-size plate of finger foods for the toddler—fries, a roll, fruit and cheese. Rose carried a sippy cup of milk in her chubby fist.

"Go on, eat. I really don't mind." She kissed Rose's forehead, brushed back her baby curls with her hand, and sat in the chair next to Easton. Bouncing her knee up and down, she began to sing softly to Rose. Melting his heart with every movement. And Rose... She looked so happy in Maureen's lap. So natural—as if they'd spent a lifetime together and this was routine.

His in-laws said nothing, looking at each other sidelong before heading to the buffet across the massive dining area, two more volunteers gathering up plates to head out the French doors to the lanai—Don and his wife always stayed late, such loyal helpers using their retirement to give back to the community. Lips tight, Delilah shoved up from the table to refill her plate, her husband following her. To keep the peace?

Draining his glass of wine, Xander let out a long sigh, eyes still fixated on Maureen, completely preoccupied as she adorably moved her mouth to create an exotic bird noise. Easton fished a toy bird out of his pocket.

Portia leaned toward Xander, following his gaze. "They're not like us."

"Are you saying Maureen belongs with him and not with me?" he asked softly.

His brother's assistant sipped her glass of wine, her voice low, as well. "No, just that they're alike in spirit."

"In spirit? I'm a man. Speak in less woo-hoo kind of terms." The idea that Maureen would be better suited for Easton set Xander's skin on fire. The suggestion bothered him more than it should have.

"I mean we're the organized, feet-on-the-ground sorts. They're the dreamers." She gestured with her wineglass, as if pointing to the vastness of space.

"They're scientists." He raised a brow at her. Scientists and dreamers didn't seem to go hand in hand. Too poetic.

"They're Dr. Doolittles. They talk to the animals and live on different plains than you and I. They don't care about convention or practicality. Their hearts are huge and defy practicality or reason. They're different."

And it was that difference that set him ablaze. But he saw his opening—the way to announce the arrangement. With his father-in-law in earshot, Xander said, "If you're congratulating me on the engagement, this is a strange way to go about it."

"Engagement?" Portia squeaked.

He cocked an eyebrow, glancing around the room quickly to see if anyone else had overheard.

Portia held up a hand and quieted her voice again. "Who am I to say anything about secret relationships? We all have our private lives."

Secret relationships? What could she possibly mean by that? Had people speculated that Maureen and he were…together before this? How would his in-laws feel if they caught wind of that? The last thing he needed was more tension or trouble from them.

Before giving any more thought to Portia's comment, his eyes fell back to Maureen a few chairs down at the lengthy table.

Out of her chair now, she raised Rose to the ceiling, simulating a plane sound. His baby girl's peal of laughter warmed the room.

Tipping her head to the side, Portia added, "Maureen's quite lovely."

"Yes, she is." Lovely. Unpredictable. Sexy. And the perfect business partner for this arrangement.

"Treat her well when you take her shopping for the ring."

"Why are you telling me this?"

"You'll have to sort that out for yourself. Besides, you're the boss. I wouldn't presume to give you advice." She smiled.

"Even if I asked for it?"

"No need to ask." She tapped his phone. "Add more features to your data planner and you can just look up the answers."

Maureen cut into the snapper with practiced ease, balancing Rose on her lap. Shoveling the fish into her mouth, she enjoyed the savory fusion of lemon, garlic and pepper.

A few bites later she felt satiated and cut up the biscuit on Rose's plate, feeding her small pieces. Rose devoured the food. *Sweet girl.* The return of her appetite said good things about her recovery.

Though she'd played it smoothly, entering with Rose on her hip, Maureen's nerves pulsated in her chest. All throughout dinner she'd felt the gaze of Xander's in-laws. As she cut up Rose's food, she could practically hear their running commentary assessing how well she was doing.

Rose lifted her small, chubby fingers, stretching and grasping toward her uncle. She squirmed in Maureen's lap, eyes fixated on Easton.

"Mmmmmmmmmmmm," Rose blurted, bouncing more emphatically.

"Easton, I think you are being summoned," Maureen said, planting a kiss on the toddler's blond hair.

Easton turned, setting his plate down at the table. A little giggle emanated from Rose as Easton stuck out his tongue at her, his voice descending into a wild birdcall.

"I'll take her from you." Easton scooped Rose up off of Maureen's lap, zooming her like a rocket ship. Hardly the normal dinner-side antics, but Easton's free spirit was what made him a brilliant boss.

"Go on, Maureen, get seconds. Thirds. Tenths. Enjoy yourself, will ya?" Easton sat in the chair next to her. "You barely put anything on your plate."

She shrugged. The few bites she'd eaten had been enough. Her nerves were starting to get the better of her. "I'm fine, Easton. But thank you. I'm going to put my plate away."

"Suit yourself."

Maureen pushed out from her chair, eyes locking with Xander's. His blue gaze sent electricity into the core of her being. Grabbing her plate from the table, she arched her eyebrow at him, hoping he would understand.

They needed to talk. So much felt up in the air. Not that Maureen wasn't up for adventure, but she could use some bearings at this point.

She maneuvered past the conversations taking place in the dining room, entering the kitchen. Scraping the food bits off her plate into the kitchen sink, she took a steadying breath. Running the water from the faucet, she flipped on the garbage disposal.

The grinding noise stifled Xander's footfalls, but Maureen saw him in the reflection of the big window. Even in a shadowed, distorted form, he sent butterflies leaping down her spine.

"So…" His voice was a sexy growl. "You're fully on board with my proposal, then?"

Turning off the water, she grabbed an orange-colored plush towel, leaning against the counter. "Tentatively."

"Tentatively? What can I do to persuade you more fully?" He took a step toward her with a smoldering smile.

She bit her lip. "More defined terms would be a decent start." Maureen couldn't let this devilishly handsome, tall, dark and sexy thing derail her from getting to the truth.

"Hmm. Well. As my wife, you'd get to stay in the States. Continue working for my brother and doing your job here, at the refuge."

"Right. That's my benefit. What do you get? Exactly?" She pinned him with a stare.

"You'd have to help me at the fundraisers, mix and mingle at work events. A stable parental figure for Rose—" he stepped closer, lowering his voice "—and a way to keep my in-laws from taking my daughter. It's not forever. Just for a bit. Until everything settles down on both our ends."

Maureen pressed her palms into the cool granite countertop, leaning back. Considering.

"I know how it sounds. But we don't have the luxury of time." Another step toward her.

Cocking her head to the side, she crossed her arms. "We don't?"

"Your work visa is going to expire. My in-laws want Rose. If it's going to happen, we can't afford to delay. We have to close the deal. Now."

Pursing her lips, she took a step toward him. "Is this how you close all your boardroom meetings?"

The heat between them was nearly tangible. Her face was inches from his.

A haughty laugh crinkled his expression. "Things don't have to stay so…businesslike. Not if you don't want them to."

She swallowed, eyes lingering on his lips. Damn. She wanted to grab him, pull him close. Feel him against her. "So you're saying, we can get engaged, married, and...explore?"

"Explore the heat between us...see where it takes us." He drew closer, lips barely brushing hers as he spoke. The smell of sandalwood anchored her. Maureen's heart thudded. She wanted him. Bad.

"I can see where this takes us."

He touched the side of her face, running a finger down her neck. "So is that your final answer?"

Her mind wandered away from the kitchen. What would it be like to be with—even if only fake married—a man that made her so reckless with her heart? The heat between them made her want to damn caution and practicality.

"My final answer? I'll do it."

As the lightning feathered across the sky, Maureen realized there was nothing typical about a date with Xander. The first indication of his adventurous nature evidenced by an impromptu date night to Miami. Via private jet. Just the two of them.

That level of grandeur had been offset by the burgeoning storm. Even that had a certain charm to it. He seemed willing to risk, to push. So different from the life she'd had when she'd been married. Everything had been dictated for her, controlled and regimented.

No, Xander reminded her of the storm outside. Full of life and flash. A force to be reckoned with. She liked this aspect of his personality.

The dark sky didn't bother her one bit. Tropical

rains were standard South Florida fare. So much for the sunshine state. And this tropical depression didn't warrant any kind of alarm. She'd quickly adopted the South Florida vibe that if you buckled down for every tropical depression, you'd never get a damn thing done. The only time to become concerned was when the bad weather turned into a tropical storm or hurricane. Not that she'd experienced either, but tropical depressions had seemed relatively minor in damages and stress.

Peeling her eyes away from outside the limo's tempered glass, her thoughts drifted back to Rose and Xander.

Rose's need for stability had lit a maternal instinct in Maureen. Sure, she'd always had a penchant for lost souls, the ones that wandered. But this was different. She'd seen Xander with his daughter, knew that the best place for Rose was with him.

So when Xander had asked her to go with him to Miami on his business jet to further stage the ruse of their engagement, she'd accepted.

Of course, that didn't mean the idea of deceiving his in-laws and the government sat well with her, but she also couldn't imagine Rose being taken from her father, from her home.

Maybe it was more Maureen's own history unsettling her. A false engagement and marriage gave her the same sort of feeling she'd gotten when she'd been talked into skydiving. The rush of adrenaline and exhilaration coalescing with fear.

He'd insisted on dinner in Miami at an upscale restaurant, Bella Terre.

He'd left his in-laws to watch Rose. And, he had admitted on the flight over, he'd left Easton and Portia to watch Delilah and Jake. An insurance that nothing would go wrong—at least nothing that his in-laws could use in a custody dispute. After spending dinner with them last night, Maureen understood and shared his concerns. They clearly loved Rose, but they wanted to manage her.

The limo stopped in front of Belle Terre, rain streaming and pooling against the window. The chauffeur popped open the door, extending a sturdy hand. He helped her out of the car, giant umbrella already extended overhead. In an instant Xander's body pressed against hers, the warmth of him teasing her senses to life as he took the umbrella from the driver and offered her his arm. She couldn't deny how damn sexy he looked, all dark-haired and charming.

As they stepped into Belle Terre, the sound of a Spanish guitar flooded her ears. Not a murmur, not a whisper or a trill of laughter pushed against the sound waves. What? That didn't make sense. Scanning the floor of the restaurant, she realized they were the only ones there. Aside from the waitstaff, of course.

Xander's breath whispered against her ear. "I rented this place. Just for us."

Her breath caught, drinking in the crystal chandelier, the rich, gold chairs.

The whole place looked like a fairy tale. Lace lingered against the white tablecloths, and as they made their way to the center of the room, she noticed the guitarist off in the corner.

He'd pulled out all the stops. So much effort, but she felt out of place in this extravagance. As he pulled her chair out for her, the scent of his woodsy cologne danced in the space between them. His fingers brushed against her bare shoulder and she stole an appreciative glance at the way his tailored suit hinted at his broad, muscular chest. Touching a hand to her neck, she fumbled with the small, teardrop-diamond necklace that rested at the center of her collarbone. The necklace, her mother's, was the finest thing she owned, and added glamour to her simple floor-length black-chiffon dress.

"You didn't have to go to all of this trouble. I already agreed to your plan."

"This engagement is going to come out of the blue. If we want people to believe we're in love, if we want to convince them all, then we need, well—" he spread his arms wide "—moments like this."

"Why not just make them up? We could get our stories together."

A true fiction uncomplicated their arrangement. But being here with him pushed up her attraction to him, made her remember the press of his body at the dance, on the beach.

Those were the kinds of feelings that needed to stay leashed to ensure the success of their deal.

As if in answer, ripples of thunder filled the room,

reminding her to stay focused. A tropical depression didn't cause the damage of a hurricane. And those memories of how he felt against her? Potentially devastating.

His eyes glinted like sexy shards of lightning snapping across the table. "You must confess, this is easier and a helluva lot more fun."

She averted her gaze, tearing away from the heat of his eyes. *Focus elsewhere. Fast.* Staring at the plate of lavish food the waiter set in front of her, Maureen's stomach leaped in anticipation. Lobster. Escargot. Shrimp. "It is lovely."

"You're lovely."

"I don't smell of fish and I'm not wearing scrubs. It's likely the contrast." Her mouth dry, and needing to divert his attention, she speared a shrimp with her fork.

"What about the night you danced by the fire? I've seen you dressed up before." Flashes of the dance materialized before her eyes. Maureen wanted to press into the simplicity of that moment.

"True." She reached for her chardonnay. A sip—then two—later, she turned to stare out the window, watching the rain bubble on the thick cut of glass.

"And I noticed then. I also noticed when you were waterlogged in the swamp covered in seaweed." He refilled his wineglass.

She smiled for an instant before her mood darkened. "And your in-laws arrived. It must be difficult for them seeing you engaged again."

"They'll have to get used to it since we will be

married soon. Very soon. The custody battle out-
weighs their personal reactions." He broke the shell
of his lobster easily. "And we'll have much to look
forward to with the refuge expanding."

As Xander continued to talk about plans for the
coming year, her stomach knotted until she barely
noticed what she ate. What type of wedding was he
going to want? Her mind skated back to her own first
marriage, that day in a massive church when she'd
expected her vows to last forever.

Xander stroked a finger across her forehead.
"Smooth that frown away. Only happy thoughts tonight. This is a new start for both of us," he said in a
way that was completely truthful regardless of who
listened in.

The waiter, a short man with a mustache like the
Monopoly game banker, removed their dinner plates
with a great flourish. In exchange, he brought molten
chocolate cake to the table, served along with two
gleaming silver forks.

"Happy thoughts. Of course." She forced a smile.
"You're right, and you've gone to so much trouble,
I must seem a horrible ingrate."

His fork edged into the chocolate cake, the melted
fudge trickling out onto the plate.

Though she felt full, a small indulgence of chocolate seemed like the right call. A spoonful of sugar to
help the deception go down. Or something like that.

"Maureen, stop worrying about what I think. Let's
focus on you. And more thoughts about how beau-

tiful you are now, and with that seaweed, and when you wear surgical scrubs."

Her shoulders rolled with her laughter. "You're quite a charmer."

"Not really. Not usually." He reached across the table to twine one of her curls around his finger. "You make it easy."

He tugged her toward him ever so gently. More thunder rolled.

"I'm not exactly a girly girl."

"You are entirely feminine. Alluring. Sexy."

Confused and more than a little rattled, she sagged back in her seat. He tugged her lock of hair ever so slightly before he let go. Were the compliments just for show? She was attracted to him and he knew it. Would he take advantage of that to enhance their ruse? She hated to think of all this male seductiveness serving as gossip for the waitstaff.

The cake lay in ruins on the plate. A bite left. Maybe two. He scooped up the last bit onto his fork. Lifted it to her lips. She took the cake off the fork, her eyes trained on his.

A small smile played on his lips and he snapped his fingers.

On cue, men in tuxedos and women in plain black dresses wheeled out carts that glittered like water in subdued light. Rows of velvet-lined cases glittered with wedding rings. Scores of them, each prettier than the last. Pressing a napkin to her mouth, she dabbed at any chocolate residue.

Was this actually happening?

Xander pushed back his chair and held out a hand for her to stand. "Choose whatever ring you want."

She pressed her fingers to her racing heart. "I couldn't do that."

"Of course you can." He took her hand and squeezed gently, tugging her upward.

"There's no need for you to go to such expense—" In fact, the amount of carats that surrounded her caused her anxiety. Too much. It was all too much.

"Expense is not an issue." He waved his hand.

"Or you could choose. Then I won't feel guilty." Heat torched her cheeks and she could almost feel her freckles popping all the more hotly to the surface.

He slid his arm around her bared shoulders until his mouth brushed her ear. "The waiters and jewelry staff have ears. Learn to be a better actress, my love."

He nipped her earlobe and she battled a wave of heat that was only partly from all that raw masculine appeal. Be a better actress? Oh, the man was getting away with too much. She simmered silently even as her body hummed from his touch. "Now, what engagement ring would you like?" he pressed, his voice sending pleasant shivers down her spine. "With a wedding band, too, of course. Let's make this a night to remember."

Two could play at this game, damn him. He wanted an act? She turned her face and nibbled his bottom lip, releasing slowly. "If you insist, *my love.*"

His gaze tracked the movement of her mouth in a telltale sign that shot a thrill through her.

For a moment they stayed there, breathing one

another's air. Locked in the drumroll moment, heat and fire building, the Spanish guitar swelling to an aching crescendo. His hand went to her jaw, his touch setting her ablaze, that familiar pull between them descending over her.

She knew then that she was no match for him in this seductive game. Her heart beat so fast she swore he must've heard it.

Her lips touched his in a perfect meet, in a kiss igniting all the sparks she had been trying to ignore for weeks. Longer even? Now those feelings flamed to life, fast and hot, coaxing a delicious warmth at just a stroke of his hand up her spine.

The glide of his mouth over hers, the parting his lips. An invitation she couldn't resist.

Five

This kiss fired his blood.

Her lips pressed into his, tongue searching and meeting until he already throbbed in response. He'd known she would be hot, that there was a connection, but this was so much more than he'd been prepared for. On instinct, his hands leaped to the back of her head, cradling and holding the kiss that seemed to kick up a notch with every passing moment.

Xander tasted her greedily, as if she might fall away off the earth if he slowed. And he had no intention of slowing. Not anytime soon.

But then a clap of thunder, one that sounded overhead, grounded him. Reminded him that they were in a restaurant. That there were boundaries in place.

He could—and would—have more of her later.

Another crack of thunder, more intense than the last. It reverberated through him, blending with his pulse. Pushing him. He felt a storm rage in his chest, building with intensity, building to get his hands on Maureen.

Xander cradled her face in his hands, passion still pumping through his veins. "How did any man ever let you go?"

A slight retreat shone in her eyes. So quick, he'd almost missed it as she spoke. "Why does anyone get divorced?"

"You don't need to brush off the statement. I'm serious. You're an incredibly smart, fascinating, sexy woman."

"I appreciate you saying that. And I could feel that attraction a few seconds ago." Her voice turned husky and low, eyebrows arching.

He liked her this way—fiery and challenging. She'd been so quiet at the beginning of dinner he'd wondered where this strong, determined woman had gone. She seemed overwhelmed by the more traditional, lavish gestures, and he'd made note. Next time, he would try to find a way to romance her that was more in keeping with her hands-on, passionate personality.

"That's more than attraction. It's damn near twenty-four-seven fascination." And even that description felt like an understatement. He drew his chair closer to hers.

"The feeling is mutual." With preternatural grace, she grazed her fingertips along the top of his thigh.

Tempting. He eased back into his chair. "I'm seriously trying to talk here."

"And I'm trying to distract you from discussion." She scrunched her nose.

"Why?"

"I don't want this to get complicated," she said tightly, easing back. "We've made it clear this is a deal."

He angled his head to the side, his eyes narrowing. "What happened to make you so closed off, so defensive?"

"Are you calling me insecure?" A hint of her Irish brogue slipped out. Exotic and powerful.

"If I wanted to use the word 'insecure,' I would have."

A moment passed. The world so still as she considered him, and in the spaces between breath, he could hear the steady drumbeat of the rain.

She bit her lip, looked him up and down, then eased back, relenting. "I shouldn't have snapped." She gestured around the dining room. "You've made everything so lovely tonight."

The hint of insecurity in her tone felt foreign to him. Maureen always had an air of confidence to her actions, even her subtle movements. Had this layer of vulnerability always been there, somehow latent and overlooked?

"Maureen, snap all you want. If I say something that upsets you, let me know. Fire up that Irish temper."

"That's a stereotype."

"Not with you."

Her lips pursed tight.

"What did I say wrong?" The evening was devolving before his eyes. He needed to figure out how to diffuse this. "Maureen? Tell me."

Leaning back in her chair, she loosened a chest-heaving breath. "I don't want to be the bitter woman who talks crap about her ex until other people yawn or run for the hills."

"You aren't. For that matter, I can't recall hearing you say anything more than irreconcilable differences."

"It was. Totally irreconcilable. I thought when we said 'till death do us part, in sickness and in health,' that's what it meant. He apparently thought it just meant until you get on my nerves and I'm just not 'happy.'" She glanced up. "I told you I can sound bitter."

"That had to be hard, having someone you love walk away for no tangible reason. He sounds like an ass."

He wanted her to know that he would never judge her for any degree of bitterness about someone so willing to walk away. That wasn't his style.

"He was an ass. Which makes me feel worse for putting up with a man who belittled me that way. The more he criticized me about getting on his nerves, the harder I worked to make him happy and the more he complained." She drew circles on Xander's shoulder absently. "I guess neither of us was very happy."

"I refer back to my original statement about him being an ass."

"There are two sides to every breakup and I'm sure he has his." Her gaze went past him, far past him. As if she was imagining how that breakup might be partly her fault. Taking the blame and somehow internalizing it.

"I've watched you this past year with the animals, with my daughter—hell, even with the way you put up with my brother. You're a good person."

"Thank you." She swallowed hard. "That means a lot to me."

"You deserve to hear it often."

"I definitely don't want to sound pathetic." Her hands flew to the sides of her temples, red curls twining around her fingers.

"You don't. You sound caring. You are kind." He cupped the back of her neck, his thumb caressing her cheek. "And you are very sexy."

"As are you." The more familiar smile and lightness edged back into her voice.

"Even if I'm all buttoned up and not the type to wade around with alligators?"

"I've seen you work with a diaper. That's far more impressive—and fearsome." Her freckled nose crinkled.

"I would have to agree. Scary stuff."

Her shoulders braced as if she'd been waiting for the right moment to broach a difficult topic. "I do want to be clear, just because we're engaged and that kiss was…undeniably full of toe-curling chemistry, that doesn't mean we'll automatically be sleeping together."

"I can't say I'm not disappointed. But then, I did state this is a marriage of convenience. When we have sex is your call." This whole marriage proposal was surreal enough for him when he'd expected to stay single for life. But he couldn't deny the lust he felt for Maureen, and the timing was right for them to help each other.

"If," she said. "If we have sex." The defiance and correction felt loaded with electricity.

A practical challenge he wanted to meet. "When."

His hand wandered back over her cheek. She leaned into his touch, eyes fluttering shut.

He brought his lips just out of reach of hers and he felt the sigh ripple from her body to his. "Time to choose your ring."

Helping her up from the table, they walked past the rows of diamonds. He watched her expression as she studied the options. Her eyes seemed to linger on a pear-shaped diamond. A pause he caught. She pushed past that ring and pointed to a small, round diamond. Traditional. Plain. The smallest one of all the ring cases.

"This one is beautiful," she said, smiling. She sent a small eye flick back to the case where the pear-diamond ring sparkled.

"Anything for you, my love." He gestured to the attendant. "We'll take the pear ring from case number three. The one in the middle."

Maureen's face flushed as the man handed Xander the ring she'd been eyeing.

He knelt down, sliding the ring on her thin finger. Eagerly, he put his lips to her finger, kissed the placement, then her wrist. When he stood, he kissed her gently on the cheek, wanting the moment to be special for her. And also knowing that if he went further, he might lose control altogether.

He pushed aside memories of Terri and what they'd shared. He had to. This was too important for his daughter.

Maureen's eyes were soft. Words seemed to press at her mouth, but found no audible track.

A familiar sound pushed against his pocket. His brother's ringtone. Immediately, Xander reached for his phone, hoping Rose was okay.

"Easton? Is Rose all right?"

Maureen's face grew pale so Xander put the phone on speaker.

Easton continued, "She's fine. But the weather's been upgraded to a tropical storm and it's predicted to be a bad one. You need to get the plane off the ground right away while it's still safe, if you plan to come home, which I assume you do. We really need your and Maureen's help to lock down the clinic and deal with any aftermath at the refuge."

Damn it. These kinds of storms could wreak havoc on wildlife, something Maureen understood, as well, as she was already reaching for her purse.

Xander extended a hand to her as he finished with his brother. "Say no more. We're leaving now."

* * *

The return flight left Maureen wrestling with a tangle of ragged nerves and stress. Was it crazy of her to be just a little bit grateful for the storm because it had distracted them from the attraction raging as fiercely as the winds outside the jet? Of course. And yet she couldn't deny as much anxiety about her feelings for Xander as she experienced about the worsening weather. The turbulence and reality of a storm coming for their refuge left her queasy and uneven.

When they'd made it back to the house, Xander's in-laws were gone. Easton said they'd blamed their departure on the weather, but they'd been upset over Xander and Maureen's engagement. Not that she could blame them.

She didn't have long to consider their reaction, though. They didn't have long to secure all the animals. Hurrying into her office, Maureen changed quickly out of her evening gown into pants and a shirt she kept stashed in a locker, piling her flowing hair into a tight ponytail.

Randy cawed from his perch, his feathers ruffling when the thunder boomed loudest. She spoke softly to him as she grabbed a rain poncho on the way out the door.

Xander and Easton were already pulling tarps over a few cages that could remain outside under the deep eaves of one of the buildings, leaving enough of a gap at the bottom to ensure fresh air even as the tarps kept out the more severe weather.

The three of them moved silently through the yard, reaching the main animal shelter.

Wind whipped at her, stinging her cheeks. So there was a huge difference in pure fury between a tropical depression and a tropical storm.

On rote memorization, she secured the animals. Talked to them in soothing tones.

Putting the storm shutters down in the avian center, the feel of the cool metal of her engagement ring pressed on her finger.

An odd feeling, really. After her divorce, her finger had ached in her wedding band's absence. So much had been promised with that little piece of metal. When she'd taken it off after her divorce, the ring's absence had left her with a lot of questions.

The clang of her ring sparked something in her. It felt strange to have another promise around her finger. At least she knew the bounds of this one.

While wings flapped nervously and the new arrivals squawked unhappily, Maureen checked all the birds, making sure they had food and water to tough out the hours of a tempest's barrage.

Through the sheeting rain, she could hear Easton trying to coax one of the big cats into the sheltered portion of their habitat, but Sheekra wasn't having it. Most cats hated the rain, but the cougar liked to sit in a tree during a storm. Xander was latching the door to the coyote shelter while Maureen dragged some of the goat feed under cover so it wouldn't spoil. Once the animals in the clinic and outdoor sanctuaries were secured, the trio raced back to the house to the storm shelter, rain pelting furiously on their backs, urging them inside.

Dripping wet, they made their way to the shelter at the center of the main house on stilts, which was protected from rising tides and secured from glass breaking through. As they ran, water puddled behind them.

Easton tossed towels at Maureen and Xander. She pressed the fabric to her face, mopping water beads that clung to her skin.

She glanced around the storm shelter. Rose sprawled on Elenora's lap, fast asleep as her sitter dozed lightly in a fat rocking chair. Looking at the child, Maureen could have almost forgotten the storm outside. The little girl epitomized peace.

The well-equipped room featured a few sofas, a generator and a fridge filled with drinks. A shelving unit pressed against the back wall was stocked with a variety of food. A reminder that these were the other kinds of dangers of living in Florida. Natural predators aside, the weather could turn life-threatening.

Easton weaved past Maureen to Portia. She sat at a table, pencil pushed into her hair, papers scattered in front of her. They began talking quietly, inventorying the status of the refuge.

Xander motioned for Maureen to join him on the blue-and-white-striped overstuffed sofa.

A crash that cut to Maureen's core pulsated above them. A low whistling sound seemed to respond. Destruction. This was the sound of destruction.

Her body shook of its own accord.

Xander pointed to the well-secured windows and the supplies. "You're okay here in the storm shelter. This place is solid. We have a top-notch generator."

Did she really look as shaken as she felt? "I understand in theory. And I researched all about hurricanes and tropical storms before I moved here, even after, because of the care needed for the animals. I just didn't expect it to be so…much."

So much? Ha. That was an understatement. From beyond the walls of the storm shelter, she heard the sounds of branches scraping against the house. The burnt smell of up-close lightning wafted into the room.

"You don't need me to tell you this isn't even the worst." That casual feeling about storms in South Florida left her. Pressing herself into him, she let his presence steady her.

The warmth of his strong arms slowed her racing pulse and helped her to take a deep breath. "Thanks."

"No problem." He tucked her closer, his soft cotton work shirt carrying a hint of his scent—a blend of something smoky and sandalwood.

"I can't believe Rose is sleeping right through this." Safer to think about his daughter than the way he smelled, even if it made Maureen want to bury her nose in his shirt.

"Storms are soothing for some. Lucky for us, she's one of those people." He rubbed Maureen's arm, his touch steady and sure. "You should try to rest, too. There will be a lot of work to do afterward, cleaning up and taking care of trapped and displaced animals."

A reminder that straightened her spine.

"And that's the reason I didn't let the storms scare me away. There's a challenge and a need here. A lot to be learned and good work to be done." How were the animals doing? Concern for them ripped through her soul. She might not like the storm, but she could rationalize it. But the animals? They didn't have that benefit.

"True enough." His voice seemed distant, and his attention drew away from her. She could feel it in the way he shifted on the sofa.

"Is there a problem?"

"I'm just thinking, remembering."

"About when your wife volunteered here."

He nodded. The pain of her absence visibly hit him as his eyes lingered on Rose.

"She wasn't scared at all, was she? Her daughter's just like her." A palpable thunder rattled through Maureen.

"Terri grew up in Florida. We all did. So while we have a healthy respect for the fickle weather, we understand it."

The internalized environment. It made sense to her. The cold of Ireland, the natural state of overcast skies and misting rain. It was a part of her. So she understood how his environment molded him. How could it not?

A crash seemed to shake the shelter. Perhaps a

tree falling? It sent her closer to him, to the muscled planes of his chest. His arms pulled her close.

They were a hairbreadth apart. Lips so close. Just like they'd been in the restaurant. All she wanted was to lose herself in him, indulge in more kisses and enjoy the bliss of that courtship of the mouths, something she'd lost over the span of a controlling and ultimately loveless marriage. She wanted to have the storm fade as she found courage to trust in his embrace.

But with so many people here with them, she held herself at bay.

Rose awoke to what Xander had identified as a falling tree. She was bleary-eyed, calm, but definitely awake.

Maureen had taken some animal figurines off the shelves and brought them to the floor. Rose climbed into her lap, clearly interested in the menagerie.

His daughter. Maureen. What a sight. Long red curls curtained the little girl's face as she played. Maureen's knees bracketed her and Rose used a chubby hand to steady herself on one of Maureen's legs.

He couldn't keep himself from thinking about Terri, though. His thoughts fell back to his life with the wife he'd lost. On the future he'd imagined for them since they were kids. She'd left him. Not by choice, of course, but her absence created a space in his life that, even fourteen months later, he felt.

Phantom pain encircled him the way an amputee still felt a missing limb.

More than that, though, he'd lost his mother shortly after. Not in a permanent, delineated way like with Terri. Growing up, Xander and Easton had been well-traveled, following his parents on adrenaline-fused adventures. Adventures that made him feel like the world had magic in it. When Xander's father died in a mountain climbing accident, his mother had been like a ball that suddenly lost its tether. She'd skidded and skirted out of his life. Hadn't even checked on him when Terri died. Wasn't there for him. Or Rose. She'd simply checked out, a bohemian spirit that refused to settle. Another fracture, another point of departure that ripped into his soul.

He didn't want anyone else leaving his life.

Under no circumstances could that happen with Maureen.

Rose's infectious laughter colored the room. Easton and Portia and some of the other staff stirred from sleep.

"Shh-hh. Shh-hh. We have to make quiet noises. What sound does this snake make?" Maureen asked, lifting a rubber snake in front of Rose.

"Hisssssss," Rose said proudly, taking the fake snake in her hand. She wriggled it in the air.

Xander moved from his chair to sit on the ground in front of her. "You're good with her."

Maureen flashed a smile his way. "Thank you."

"I know I've indulged her."

She stayed quiet.

"Okay, I've spoiled her."

Maureen shook her head, giving Rose a quick hug. A grin bloomed across the toddler's mouth. "You've loved her. She lost her mother. She needed to feel secure and she's attached to you."

"And she's spoiled."

"And you'll do something about that at the right time." She handed Rose a rubber tiger. The baby made a growling noise.

"You handle her tantrums well."

"I'm not her parent."

"Her boo-boo lip protruding doesn't move you the way it tears me apart." And it did. All that talk about being able to resist his little girl's charm had cracked.

"It moves me. I just—" she shrugged "—think it's easier for me to be the bad guy."

"That's a nice way to put it. I'm working on it, though. I have to. I'm just still finding my footing on parenting. It's tougher than I could have known. I don't want to spoil her, but I want her to feel loved and confident."

"For what my opinion is worth, I think you're doing a great job. Every child deserves as good." A heavy sigh passed through her and her gaze fell away from his with hesitancy and resignation. He recognized that look. Had seen Terri exhibit a similar reaction.

"Your parents were critical?"

"Strict. The divorce was difficult for them to accept." Maureen's normally full lips thinned.

"I'm sorry. You deserved support."

"Thank you for the sympathy but, honestly, it made me stronger in the end. I'm here, forging a new path."

This woman embodied resilience. He admired her for that. Wanted to drink that into his essence. Starting a new path wasn't easy. Especially when he'd thought his life had been planned out.

"I'm sorry the stress of getting engaged to me brought back bad memories." He hadn't anticipated what it might be like for her, his plans taking shape around his own needs and a desire to keep her working at the refuge.

"Nothing to apologize for. You're saving me from having to give up the work I love. Thank you for filing the paperwork so quickly." She heaved a sigh of relief. "You kept me from having to go back to all the reasons I left in the first place."

"Are you hiding here until you're ready to return?" Maybe the question wasn't fair. But he needed to understand her motivations. Maureen's veiled past made it difficult to understand her full perspective.

"Hiding? That's a harsh word. I'm not sure if I plan to go back. I just know my destiny is here for now."

Stroking Rose's feathery hair, she added, "One day at a time."

Perhaps that sentiment was her marching orders. Kept her from feeling the weight of forever.

"Fair enough." His hand found hers and he stroked her palm, his thumb moving along the band of the ring he'd placed there what felt like another world ago. He could sense her tiredness, her fraying. "Do you mind if I ask you one last question?"

She eyed him warily. "Okay, shoot."

"Can you help teach me that trick for getting my daughter to stop pitching a temper tantrum?" He tried for levity, adding in a grin for good measure.

Her shoulders lifted with her laugh. A good sound. A needed one. He had this well in hand, damn it. Friendship and attraction. Just that. Good. Satisfying. Not dangerous, not something that would shatter his world again.

"I'll try my best." She took Rose's hand in hers and played with her pinky finger. "But I suspect we may have to work on how tightly she has you wrapped around that tiny finger of hers."

"You may have a point."

The still room seemed to inhale and hold its breath. Everyone slept. His eyes met hers and her lips parted slightly. His desire and longing for her returned.

They were engaged now and kissing her would sell the cover story even more. But beyond cementing their story, he wanted to feel her against him. Craved it. Ached to have her in bed, to be inside her, to wake up with her next to him and see all that magnificent red hair splayed across the pillow.

He nearly took his chance on his wife-to-be but then the radio blurted emergency signals.

The room burst into life as the radio host gave an update on the tropical storm. The worst had passed them by, moving on toward Miami. They could re-enter the main part of the house now.

And maybe even find some privacy.

Six

The tropical storm had ruffled the landscape of the refuge. Xander surveyed the grounds, noting the damage. An uprooted tree from the east of the property found a new home just outside the bird sanctuary. Speaking of which, glass speckled the ground outside the aviary. That'd been the first place Maureen dashed to. She'd wanted to make sure those birds that couldn't survive on their own in the wild were safe.

The busted glass was thankfully the most substantial damage any of the buildings sustained. Xander made a mental note to put the hurricane shutters for the newly constructed part of the refuge on rush. The tropical storm's damage reminded him a hurricane would be devastating by comparison. They needed to make sure all of the windows were secured.

Of course, other miscellaneous pieces of shrubbery decorated the lawn. Palm fronds, bushes, branches and garbage scattered the area, looking like discarded wrapping paper after an eager child's Christmas morning.

Alongside Easton and Xander, volunteers began reclaiming the space. A crew had arrived on-site early, setting up a tent with bottled water and boxed lunches for the group, acting as command central for the cleanup efforts. By now, most of the new arrivals were either piling up debris or acting as company for some of the more unsettled animals. While cleaning up after the tropical storm frustrated him—he hated lugging and stacking branches—he'd been glad for the minimal damage. Tree branches were annoying, sure. But if they'd lost a building and the animals inside? That would be much harder to come back from.

Xander worked in silence, stacking palm fronds one on top of the other in what looked like a woodsy edition of Jenga. Easton added to the pile, too. The other volunteers spread out around the yard, giving Easton and Xander a small degree of privacy.

He'd always been close to his brother. That's how he knew Easton was weighing his approach to something he wanted to discuss. His indecision rendered itself visible in the way he carelessly tossed the branches and licked his lips.

Easton cast a sidelong glance at Xander, jaw set and voice quiet. "Are you sure you know what you're doing?"

"I can lift a branch and work a saw. It's not like I

never leave the office." He could still steer this conversation.

"That's not what I'm talking about and you know it."

Xander kept working silently. He wasn't interested in advice right now and if his brother wanted to confront him, he would have to work for it.

Easton tugged off his heavy-duty work gloves. "Come on, brother. You're not really going to pull that old silence act, are you? You pretend like I don't know you."

"Say what you want."

"You got engaged to Maureen to ensure your custody of Rose is secure."

"I'm marrying her." No discussion. Just the matter-of-fact delivery that had made him such a success in the business world. Xander chucked another piece of a palm tree onto the wobbling stack.

"For real? And what does she think about this—" He sighed. "She gets to stay in the States. Aren't you worried about the legal implications of a fake marriage?"

"It will be a real marriage." The words pressed out of his clenched teeth. This was *his* life, not his brother's. He didn't have any right to comment.

"What does Maureen think? How honest have you been with her? Because I'm not buying for a second that you're in love with her." Easton held up his hand once he saw a protest form. "Oh, I get that you're in lust with her. But love? Nope. I've seen you in love before."

Pain lanced Xander at the reminder of all he'd lost. Damn it.

"What makes you think anything Maureen and I discuss is any of your business?"

"I'm family." He folded his arms across his chest, staring.

Xander inhaled deeply, drawing closer to his brother. Undaunted. "Then be supportive, damn you."

A command and a warning all at once.

Easton nodded, but his body tightened into hard lines. "I'm your brother, so I'm the one person not afraid to stand up to you."

"Maureen and I understand each other." The arrangement benefited them both. She'd chosen to accept his offer.

"Do you realize how vulnerable she is?" Easton's octave dropped, eyes scanning Xander's.

"I know her past with her ex-husband."

"Then tread warily. Because you may be my brother but she's my friend, and if you break her heart, I will kick your ass."

"I'm not going to hurt her and you're not going to kick my ass."

"If worse comes to worst, I have the gators on my side."

He playfully slugged Xander on the shoulder before stepping away toward a group of volunteers.

Xander watched his brother walk away, but his eyes settled on Maureen. She emerged from the bird sanctuary. Hair piled high into a ponytail, gloves and trash bag in hand. Ready to work. Even now, she looked stunning. This storm-torn element reflected a truth about Maureen, he noted. That her heart sung for these moments of reconstruction, that her earthy vibe and huge heart rendered her beautiful.

His mind wandered back—had it really only been a few hours ago when she'd spoken of her ex-husband?—to the pain and calluses he'd uncovered.

He warily regarded his brother's warning about hurting her. He didn't want to be so significant to her that he could cause her emotional pain.

And yet, their engagement, his proposal…it had to be right. He needed to keep custody of Rose and Maureen needed to stay in the States. He'd put them on this course and had to see it through. They were too far in to go back now.

And besides, he wanted to take that kiss to its very satisfying conclusion in bed.

Cleaning up after the storm had left everyone sticky with sweat and dirt. In her short time in the Keys, she'd learned a shower wasn't the first way to clean up after muck and grime attached to skin. The ocean, now settled and calm, claimed the first rite of cleansing.

This system of ocean cleansing before an outright shower jibed with Maureen's sensibilities. If nothing else, it'd proved an excuse to literally immerse herself in this landscape. Two years later and Maureen still found the water enchanting. She loved how there were multiple incarnations of water on this small island. The boggy area she'd fallen into represented only part of what Key Largo offered. That swampy ecosystem supported specific types of creatures, had its own scent and flavor. And then there was the ocean access—unreal colors of turquoise sparkling in the sun. For such a small island, Key Largo's nuances fascinated her.

As she looked around, she felt suddenly aware of how the wildlife refuge had become its own ecosystem, one she felt part of. The group of dedicated volunteers who had showed up today astounded and humbled her.

They'd waded into the water, too, ready for a little bit of fun after a morning that had everyone's muscles aching. The whole area seemed alive with chatter and laughter. No one had bothered changing, charging headlong into the water, clothes and all. A minor form of recklessness she enjoyed.

Even Portia had joined in the impromptu beach excursion. Maureen watched as a wave fell against Portia's back, soaking her clothes. Easton's whooping laugh filtered on the breeze.

Maureen's breath hitched a bit as Xander approached. Self-consciously, she adjusted the strap of her green tank top. When she'd started the cleanup this morning, she'd been in a T-shirt and shorts. The Florida sun had warmed her, prompting her to discard the black shirt in favor of the tank top. Layering clothes was a leftover habit from Ireland she'd yet to break.

As he approached he discarded his shirt, tucking

it into the pockets of his shorts. Heart quickening, her eyes fell on his muscled chest. Why did he have to be so damn sexy?

His smile caught her off guard, pairing nicely with his dark hair. He had that old-school-movie-star glamour, effortless charm.

Just like that, he made his way to her. Their bodies so close. And she became aware of just how thin their physical barriers were.

She flashed him a grin as he took her hands, leading them deeper into the ocean. The small waves caused them to brush more and more against each other. And move farther away from Easton, Portia and the volunteers. A semblance of privacy.

Maureen splashed water at Xander, trying to maintain a lightness in their communication that ran counter to the unease mounting in her gut. "What a relief that we're all okay and the refuge only suffered minor damage."

"We've been lucky this hurricane season."

"I read up on the storms before moving here, preparing myself, and so far I feel over prepared."

"The time will come you'll use that knowledge, now that you're staying." His hand brushed her cheek, sending shivers down her spine. The warmth of his fingertips almost made her forget what had plagued her mind all morning during the cleanup.

She raised her eyebrows. "Maybe there won't be one during my time here, since I'm not staying permanently." Her forehead creased. "We never did talk about how long this marriage is supposed to last."

She stared down at the ring on her finger where her hand rested on his forearm, her skin so pale next to his while the diamond sparkled in the sunlight.

"We can figure that out later. This isn't the time or the place to discuss it, anyway, when someone could walk up and overhear."

"Of course, you're right." She curled her toes in the soft white sand.

He wrapped his arms around her waist. "We should be persuading people we're a couple, an engaged couple, a totally enamored couple." His hands skimmed up and down her back, inciting pleasurable shivers. "It's not that difficult to be convincing. You are a gorgeous woman, Maureen, and that smart mind of yours is every bit as sexy."

His words held her spellbound. He stared a moment at her and she felt the press of the waves knock them even closer. As if by instinct, his grip on her waist tightened. The squeeze encouraged contact, underscoring her desire to get closer. His wet thigh brushed hers, igniting a rush of longing so strong it threatened to pull her under faster than any wave.

And so she kissed him, tasting the salt on his lower lip. Warming up to this moment she'd been thinking about—no, *hoping* for—all morning. His right hand cupped her head, keeping her with him. As if she had any thought of backing away. Anticipation fired hot inside her, deep in her belly, radiating out to tremble through her limbs. Making her weak with desire.

He drank her in, pushing farther with his tongue

until the space between his body and hers melted away. So much so that they were unaware of the approaching wave.

It rocked them, pulling them gently underneath the water, but their bodies remained entwined. Eyes closed, lips still pressed together. Even with the water closing over her, the only tangible relationship was the feel of his body and hers. How she wanted to luxuriate here, in this feeling of weightlessness. To surrender full control to the moment as his body pressed more firmly to hers. Her breasts ached for his caress and she could feel him against her, broadcasting how much he wanted her, as well.

An urgency for air disrupted that need, however. They pushed their way to the surface with quick inhales.

And then he pulled her back, folding her into him. Kissing her deeply. Hungrily. The sounds of the seagulls and volunteers returning her to the moment in a way she didn't want. For a secluded refuge, there sure were a lot of people around all the time.

Don, a volunteer with spiked hair, shouted in their direction, "Get a room, you two."

She thought that sounded like a brilliant idea. And, oh, God, what was she thinking to let herself get so aroused in a public place? She could barely catch her breath.

Xander lifted an eyebrow at her. "Interested in a room?"

She splayed her hands along his chest, trying

to slow her racing heart rate. "I thought you said I would call the shots on the issue of when—or if— we sleep together."

"I did ask."

"True." She looked down at her hands, her engagement ring sparkling in the bright Florida sun, a reminder that she needed to think carefully about her decisions when it came to him. "But this is all so new to me. Let's take our time."

"Ah, the lady would like to be romanced."

She laughed lightly. "Perhaps the man should be romanced, too."

"We chase each other?"

"We do have a wedding to plan." This romance would leave her with whiplash if she wasn't careful. She needed to remain in control of the situation.

"Are you suggesting we wait until the wedding night?"

"Is that such an outrageous idea? Especially considering how quickly this all came about?"

Cupping her face, he let out a groan. "Sounds like an incredible invitation to foreplay. But keep in mind, we get married in a week."

"Not much time to plan a wedding."

He rubbed a thumb along her bottom lip. "And an eternity to get you into my bed."

Sleep held Xander in the hazy world of the past. In that most vulnerable time, when there were no safeguards in place to stop the memories that could slay a man, he was tormented by memories he'd been fighting hard since the word *marriage* became a part of his life again.

He stood at the altar of the church, eyes trained on the big oak door. Waiting for her. Anticipation of the future coloring his stance, making his heart palpitate. The moment stretched before him like an eternity. Easton leaned in next to him. "Delilah's straightening out the flowers on the pew. For the third time."

Was she? Xander hadn't even noticed. His sole focus had been on waiting for Terri to come through those doors. So they could start their lives together.

"Today I don't even care." He meant it, though he did avert his gaze to see Delilah fuss over the lilies by their parents. Xander's mother looked at him, joy painting her face in a serene, eye-shining smile. She squeezed his father's hand. Xander nodded at them, his father winking in response. Perfection. This was what it looked like.

"I know. I just thought it'd help distract you. Dude, you look intense right now." A small, nearly inaudible laugh.

"Ah. Always looking out for me, aren't—"

The doors opened. This was the moment. The organist began playing "Here Comes the Bride."

All of the air was knocked from his lungs. Terri radiated as she approached, her slender frame accented by the A-line skirt. Her blond hair styled in perfect ringlet curls.

Jake walked next to her, looking at Xander with a fierceness.

"Take care of my baby girl," he mouthed to Xander.

In response, Xander nodded. Of course he would. He'd shield her from anything.

Grasping Terri's hand, Xander had never felt more certain about anything in his life. That they'd live happily ever after. Have kids. The works.

But then she started seizing. Shaking. On the ground. Voices pushed against him.

Paramedics appeared. An aneurism. That's what they were saying.

This was all wrong. Not like this.

And it wasn't like this. Where was Rose?

He looked at Terri, her body stilling after the seizure. Life flooding out of her eyes. Pain flooding his. The pink rose she'd been holding lay limp in her hands.

He went to pick up the rose, but it fell away from his grip, becoming—

Sheets?

Blinking, Xander kicked aside the blankets in his California King bed and took in his surroundings. He heard the steady beat of waves against sand, the feel of his Egyptian cotton sheets and his tossed pillows.

A damn nightmare.

A helluva way to cap off an exhausting twenty-four-hour period. Sweat soaked his sheets and even trickled down his chest.

No way he could stay in bed after that piece of the past shredded him. Space and air. That's what he needed. Anything to get those images out of his mind.

He'd never been much of a runner. Instead he'd found swimming to be what set his mind right. In times of stress, personal or business, he'd found a few laps brought him solace.

And he needed that now.

Quietly he slipped out of his room to the grand pool. He'd brought in a special designer, wanting this to be a kind of sanctuary for Rose, too. So he'd pulled out all the stops. Salt water and Olympic length, he'd also had a faux water cliff constructed on the back wall. Waterfalls had been added, giving off a very distinct lagoon feeling. Even the hot tub had been incorporated into the tropical feeling. Live palms were interspersed in the design, shading the hot tub and adding texture to the cliff.

As he closed the sliding-glass door behind him, he noticed he hadn't been the only one with this idea.

Water rippled behind a redheaded mermaid. The hair webbing behind her, parting to reveal a topless Maureen.

While swimming topless was a European custom he appreciated, his desire ramped up. Without a second thought, he shucked his blue shorts and dove in after her.

Seven

Water flowed over Maureen's body, washing away the tension of the day, the storm. Her desire for a man still in love with his dead wife.

A man Maureen had agreed to marry.

What had she been thinking?

Why couldn't he have been a troll?

She swam harder, faster, desperate to wear herself out to the very last atom of energy so she could fall into a dreamless slumber. She was a strong swimmer, a part of not only her job but also from having grown up on the craggy shores of a waves-tossed Irish village. She wanted to swim in the ocean tonight but fear of sharks and riptides had kept her in check at the last minute, opting for the pool instead.

No one stirred this late at night, anyway. She could be alone with her thoughts.

A whoosh of water rippled over her. From the fountain or water features? She opened her eyes and realized...

Xander swam in front of her, side-stroking, studying her through the crystal waters. God, he was so muscular and broad-chested.

He matched her pace, stroke for stroke. Tendons in his arms rippled with each strong sweep through the crystal water. Definitely nothing troll-like about this man. Instead he exuded power and seduction with every ripple that broke against his tanned skin.

Not ready to come to full reality, to words, Maureen pushed on. Since their impromptu dinner at Belle Terre, they'd yet to be alone together. Even at the restaurant, waitstaff and musicians had stood at an attentive, audible distance. Now this midnight swim felt different from that night.

Cresting the water for a moment, she stole a glance at him and the lanai beyond. Alone. They were actually alone. No Easton or Portia or volunteers.

The thought simultaneously thrilled and terrified her. Never before had two equal but opposite forces begged her muscles for movement. So she kept swimming, kept doing her laps, all too aware of the throaty sound of his breathing, of his lips searching for air.

A phantom trace of the kiss from the ocean lingered in her thoughts when she pushed off the side of the pool, more determined than ever to keep swimming. As if swimming in this pool with him and not throwing herself at her very sexy, fake fiancé would prove to Maureen once and for all that she was in control.

He kept time with her. To an outsider, they must have looked like synchronized swimmers. Every so often, on the lap exchange, she'd catch his eye. A watery grin and challenge arched in his eye. They went on lapping until Maureen lost count, until her lungs and limbs burned with exhaustion. Finally, they both stopped at the side by the water feature.

Gasping, she asked, "What brought you out here tonight?"

"What brought you?" he asked back, not in the least winded, which almost made her roll her eyes but also gave her a moment of pleasure to appreciate his strength.

Treading water, she shrugged, keeping energy in her limbs. "Trouble sleeping. I guess I'm too ramped up from all the stress of the storm and cleanup. Relieved, too, but over-revved. And you?"

"The same. Adrenaline."

Xander pulled himself out over the pool's lip and into the hot tub, settling on the far wall. She followed, aware of him and appreciating the way his gaze lingered on her exposed breasts.

But the appreciation also made her aware that she needed to be more careful. Put boundaries up. Though the water teased and wrapped just above her breasts, she scanned for her bikini top. Too exposed, too quickly.

She nibbled her lip and reached for her stretchy Lycra top on the concrete. And wrapped the front tie bandeau around her again.

Xander smiled, his eyes heavy-lidded and sexy. "Damn shame to cover up such beauty."

"Someone else could be awake. I shouldn't have been so reckless. I forget I'm not in Europe sometimes."

"Well, I won't so easily be forgetting the loveliness I saw, regardless of what you're wearing." His lips tipped in a crooked grin, eyes lingering from mouth to bikini top and finally flicking back to her eyes. Rattling her to the core.

"I'll simply take that as a compliment, you wicked man." She flipped her red hair that already had begun to form little ringlets.

"I'm your wicked fiancé." He floated toward her, the movement of the water sending anticipatory chills down her spine.

"Yes, you are, and we agreed this is in name only."

She was telling it to him as much as she was telling it to herself.

"How long do you think we'll be able to hold on to that sterile farce with all this attraction and chemistry damn near electrocuting us as we sit here in the water?" He motioned lightly with his fingers in the space between them, the light tremors pressing into her chest. How she wanted him to actually

"FAST FIVE" READER SURVEY

Your participation entitles you to:
✳ **4 Thank-You Gifts Worth Over $20!**

Complete the survey in minutes.

Get **2 FREE** Books

Your Thank-You Gifts include **2 FREE BOOKS** and **2 MYSTERY GIFTS**. There's no obligation to purchase anything!

See inside for details.

Dear Reader,

Since you are a lover of our books, your opinions are important to us... and so is your time.

That's why we made sure your **"FAST FIVE" READER SURVEY** can be completed in just a few minutes. Your answers to the five questions will help us remain at the forefront of women's fiction.

And, as a thank-you for participating, we'd like to send you **4 FREE THANK-YOU GIFTS!**

Enjoy your gifts with our appreciation,

Pam Powers

To get your
4 FREE THANK-YOU GIFTS:

✶ Quickly complete the "Fast Five" Reader Survey
and return the insert.

"FAST FIVE" READER SURVEY

1 Do you sometimes read a book a second or third time?　　○ Yes　○ No

2 Do you often choose reading over other forms of entertainment such as television?　　○ Yes　○ No

3 When you were a child, did someone regularly read aloud to you?　　○ Yes　○ No

4 Do you sometimes take a book with you when you travel outside the home?　　○ Yes　○ No

5 In addition to books, do you regularly read newspapers and magazines?　　○ Yes　○ No

YES! I have completed the above Reader Survey. Please send me my 4 FREE GIFTS (gifts worth over $20 retail). I understand that I am under no obligation to buy anything, as explained on the back of this card.

225/326 HDL GKEU

FIRST NAME

LAST NAME

ADDRESS

APT.#

CITY

STATE/PROV.

ZIP/POSTAL CODE

D-816-SFF15

▲ If offer card is missing write to: Reader Service, P.O. Box 1867, Buffalo, NY 14240-1867 or visit www.ReaderService.com ▲

BUSINESS REPLY MAIL

FIRST-CLASS MAIL   PERMIT NO. 717   BUFFALO, NY

POSTAGE WILL BE PAID BY ADDRESSEE

READER SERVICE
PO BOX 1867
BUFFALO NY 14240-9952

NO POSTAGE
NECESSARY
IF MAILED
IN THE
UNITED STATES

touch her. But she needed to keep her head. For both their sakes.

"I believe sex would complicate things tremendously when we have to say goodbye."

"It doesn't have to, not as long as we agree to get on as amiably as this, friends. It could be fun, exciting... Think of the adventures we could have in this exotic locale."

Oh. Was she just a way to live out what never was with Terri? The thought gutted her like a fish at market. That would never work, not for either of them. It wouldn't be fair to Terri's memory or to Maureen's world. "I won't be a part of you replaying your past."

His face went somber. "I wouldn't dishonor either of you that way. Anything between you and me is just that, about the two of us. New experiences. New adventures."

"I want to trust that." And she did want to trust that. But, damn, their scenario exploded with complications and unhealed wounds. A dangerous combination.

"You want to trust me. You want *me*. Because I sure as hell want you."

She glanced down, his thick erection visible enough through the material of his shorts and the hot tub swirls. "I can tell."

He grinned. Definitely wicked.

She splashed him. "Wipe that look off your face."

He tossed back his head and laughed and Lord, that was every bit as enticing as his smile, his face.

His body.

"Maureen, I truly meant what I said. We'll take our time. Wanting and acting on those desires are two different things. When you're ready, clearly—" he glanced down with a wry smile "—I'll be ready, as well."

"And meanwhile?"

His thigh grazed hers. "I'll be doing my best to romance you and entice you to make that night one to remember."

The dwindling golden rays of late afternoon glinted off the deck of the glass-bottomed section of the yacht. But nothing looked more radiant than Maureen.

She stood a few feet away from him, her wild hair ablaze in the light, loose curls against ivory skin and a green shift dress. Slow, smooth jazz stirred on the breeze, coming from the small band stationed at the end of the yacht in front of the makeshift dance floor where high-powered couples pressed cheeks.

Xander watched her eyes take in the fish darting in and out of the coral. A bemused smile on her lips.

For him, this sort of gathering felt stale and stifling. At least it had for the last fourteen months. He'd always found excuses for attending the minimum amount of social gatherings since Terri's death. Too many questions. Everyone gave him a sympathetic headshake.

With Maureen by his side? Everything changed. He wanted to show her a fine evening, to romance her. She deserved that. So he'd confirmed his RSVP for the company's glass-bottomed boat charity event.

He scanned the crowd, noting the sheer variety of movers and shakers. A lot of these guys were politicians whose plastically constructed trophy wives made the Stepford wives look like a leper colony. Local celebrities from the Miami sports teams sipped champagne, huddled among the wealthiest people Miami-Dade County had to offer.

A glittering world. Xander could almost forget there'd been a tropical storm as he looked toward the shore. A few knocked and battered trees, but most of the lush greenery remained intact. A tropical oasis beckoning.

A part of him worried he was letting go of Terri's memory, yet he also couldn't help but indulge in Maureen's company that reminded him he was still alive, something he'd avoided thinking about or feeling since Terri's death.

And the people on the glass-bottomed section of the yacht were all potential partners, investors and promoters. He turned to the bartender, handing over his downed bourbon-on-the rocks glass. An older man and his wife sidled past Xander, bumping in to him.

"Oh, so sorry, love," the older lady with gray-blue hair crooned. Her voice sounded real and genuine, something often lacking at gatherings of the elite and wealthy. She and her husband looked like the kind of people he liked to chat with at events like these.

"Not a problem at all," Xander murmured, waving his hand.

Her husband, an older gentlemen dressed in a fairly modest black suit, cleared his throat. "You and your girl remind us of, well...us when we were younger. Hold on to her," he added, winking before walking away with his wife.

"Thank you, sir." Xander knew he and Maureen were selling the engaged couple act well. Truth be told, she made it damn easy. Maureen's natural beauty, her kind heart. Their intense chemistry. The role seemed like a perfect cast.

Looking back toward Maureen, he realized he wasn't the only one appreciating the way her body curved. A tall blond man approached her, eyes hungry.

A wave of jealousy coursed in Xander's blood, bubbling in his stomach. He cut the blond man off at the pass, planting a kiss on her forehead, placing his palm possessively on her spine.

"Dance with me, my love," he breathed into her ear.

She nodded, her slender hand folding in his. He pulled her to the dance floor, his hand finding purchase again along the small of her back. She was his. He didn't want to question why he felt that way, not now. He just wanted to hold on to this moment, this attraction. He just had to pick the right moment to make his move to win her over into his bed.

"You reminded me of the Little Mermaid a few moments ago."

"For real? So you've had a Little Mermaid crush since you were, like, ten years old?"

He choked on a laugh then shook his head. "Maybe. But make no mistake, my feelings now are one hundred percent adult, feeling drawn to the siren song of a luscious adult mermaid."

"For real? That's…intriguing." Her voice was a sigh on pink lips.

"Yeah. When you were standing there, looking at the fish with the coral backdrop. You looked like part of that landscape. Like I said, a siren."

"Mmm."

Her subdued response tipped him off that her mind trailed elsewhere.

"What's wrong?"

Pulling back slightly from the intimate slow dance, she squared to look at him. "This is your life? Full of parties and gatherings with the wealthiest people in the country?"

He mentally regrouped, trying to gauge where this was coming from, where it might be leading. And what that meant regarding turning the page on his past with Terri.

"I'm a person with a chance to make a difference. I do that my way. You do the same in your way."

"What about all the waste here?" Heat entered her syllables, infusing them with accusations and distaste.

"Be more specific." He couldn't address her concerns until he understood them better, but he recalled her discomfort at Belle Terre, almost as if she didn't dare enjoy the opulent dinner.

"The decadence? You know, like endless escargot and party bags with gold and sapphire jewelry."

"They chose how to spend their money and that money went into a business's pocket, feeding back into the economy. And the majority of the people on the yacht donated heavily to charity, as well." He couldn't help his defensiveness. He knew the people here could solve a lot of the world's problems with the kinds of checks they wrote. And they frequently did just that. "So your problem is?"

He glanced around the deck, taking note of Jerry Ghera, the world-famous surgeon who'd given up his private practice to be part of Doctors Without Borders. Sure, the lights, the band, the food was lavish... but a lot of these people were kind and generous.

Pausing, she nibbled her bottom lip. "I sounded judgmental, didn't I?"

"Were you being judgmental?" Every time Xander thought he'd pegged Maureen, figured her out, a surprise leaped out at him.

"What did Terri think of this lifestyle?"

The tempo quickened so he increased their pace, spinning her around and then back to him. "She wasn't comfortable in large groups."

"So it wasn't the money for her, just so many people?"

"Basically, yes. Her parents are quite well-off." A problem only because of the power that came with their wealth and what it might mean for his daughter.

He'd never given their wealth—any of the wealth— much thought before.

"I didn't realize that."

"Terri's money is all in a trust for Rose."

"And Rose's maternal grandparents?" She pressed into him, leaning in as he led her toward the center of the dance floor.

"They could pitch one helluva battle for custody of Rose if they decided to dig in deep."

The Irish anger leeched from her face. Concern touched her brow, causing it to furrow and her eyes to widen. In a lower voice, she asked, "Have they been in touch or made threats?"

"No. Nothing since our engagement announce-ment." He thrust his hand through his hair. "I want to find a way to trust them so they can spend more time with her. But I'm terrified they'll leave the country with her."

"Do you seriously think they would go to illegal lengths?"

"They loved their daughter and I understand that. God, I understand a parent's love for their kid. But Rose is my daughter. My child." He closed his eyes for a moment. There'd be time to deal with all of that later. He sighed hard before continuing. "Enough of that kind of discussion. You're supposed to be hav-ing decadent fun."

"It is a lovely party," she admitted finally, al-though it was obviously not the kind she'd ever throw.

He winked. "I enjoy the way you dance."

"Are you teasing me?" Her head tilted to the side, a strand of hair falling into her face.

Lifting his hand from her side, he tucked the curl behind her ear.

"Your moves are sexy as hell, lass. I would never tease you about that. In fact, now that I'm thinking about it, maybe I don't want them seeing you dance."

An overpowering stillness rippled through Maureen's body, like someone had fastened her with a pin like a Victorian moth. Her normal grace and fluidity vacated her features, a retreating shift he felt as tension rippled through her.

"Maureen? What's wrong?" Trying like hell to read her face, to understand what had happened.

"It's nothing." Her lip jutted, brow furrowed, and her voice sounded distant and cold. Not a terribly convincing liar.

"Clearly, it's something."

Her eyes, filled with rage and resignation, met his. "My ex had a jealousy issue. A bad one."

Damn. His brother's veiled warning about how bad her ex was entered his mind again. "Did he hurt you?"

"Physically? God, no." She held up her hands. "Forget I said anything. Really. I don't want to talk about this."

Maureen pulled back, shifting her weight onto her slender heels. Leaving the dance floor and him.

He needed her to understand that he shared little in common with her ex. He'd never been the kind of man to emotionally or physically hurt a woman. Didn't have it in him for that level of manipulation.

Determined to make his point, he searched the crowd for her until he found her chatting with a group of women around a champagne fountain. Her glorious red hair drew him like a beacon. Lightly, he touched her arm, fixing her with a stare.

A shudder unfolded beneath his fingertips, but she stayed. In the truest way he knew how to convey his understanding, he kissed her. Lightly, on the forehead. Then softer still on her mouth. The tension in her stance eased.

Xander held out his hand. "Keep dancing with me. We won't talk. Just…dance."

In response she drew closer in his arms, practically melting into his body. The light scent of her jasmine perfume enveloping him as a sigh ricocheted through her body.

Damn. This woman… She could become a living flame, and when she burned, it was bright and fearsome. He admired the hell out of her spirit. And her willingness to stay here, pressed up against him, meant he might be getting through to her. Winning her over, after all.

With a week left until the wedding, he hoped Maureen would begin to trust him. To separate him from that scumbag ex of hers. If he played all his cards right, kept that boardroom bravado, she would be his.

And he would have to learn to overcome the twinge in his gut—in his heart—that suggested he was somehow betraying Terri. Because no matter how many times he told himself he and Maureen were just helping each other out, he knew damn well he wanted her.

Wedding planning.

Words that normally involved a small group of girlfriends pouring over websites and bridal magazines, mimosas in hand. Picking out decorations that reflected the couple's collective personalities.

This meeting with Portia? Opposite of that.

Not that Maureen minded. She'd done the months-of-planning wedding before. And her real wedding had ended with real pain, despite the hours of primping and making her wedding day look like a spread in one of those magazines.

Even with Portia's assistance, and the knowledge that somehow this wedding wasn't real, she still felt nervous. For a variety of reasons.

The biggest of which? Her conflicted but ever-present attraction to her fiancé. Her *fake* fiancé. A reality that continued to crash into her soul.

"So talk to me about what you'd like your wedding to be like. The vibe you are going for. I'm great at organizing and getting things done quickly," Portia said, taking a seat next to Maureen. Portia clicked her retractable pen and wrote the wedding date at the top of her legal pad.

A week to go until the wedding. A week and nothing planned yet. *Not a big deal. Not a big deal.* If she told herself that enough times, would it become true?

"The exact opposite of my first one," Maureen quipped, folding her legs into lotus position. She ran her fingers on the light fabric of her capris, thinking back to her wedding.

"What was your first one like?" Portia asked.

A loaded question. "In a nutshell? Too big."

And not by Maureen's choice. Her parents, her now ex-husband—they'd all wanted the big white wedding. A huge bridal party, a guest list of over 200 people. A wedding dress that had practically swallowed her whole in yards of fabric. A cathedral-length train. She wanted this wedding—real or not—to feel nothing like that.

"You don't strike me as the big wedding type, anyway."

"I'm not interested in replaying the past in any capacity. Which reminds me—" a blush burned on Maureen's cheeks "—I should extend the same courtesy to Xander. Any chance you know what his wedding was like?"

Portia chewed at her lip, shaking her head. "No. Do you want to call and ask him?"

Oh, heavens no. Maureen had to think quickly on her feet. "I don't want to bother him at the office."

Portia laid the pen to the center of her chin. "We could always look at his wedding album. It's in the family room."

"Great. That'd be perfect." Maureen exhaled a little too quickly. Portia's eyebrows inclined slightly, but she didn't press.

"I'll be right back." Portia set her pad and pen on

the driftwood coffee table, flitting out of the room. Moments later she returned, album in hand.

Moving the chairs together, Portia and Maureen sifted through the album. For a moment Maureen felt intrusive, looking at these photos.

Her heart burst as she took them in. His smile, bright, unfettered by heartbreak. She wished he could still look like that, feel like that. Terri and Xander had been a beautiful couple. Their wedding, also very traditional, had been set in a large church.

"Oh, look at Easton," Portia said, laughing at the picture of Easton dancing next to Xander's in-laws. Always a ham.

Maureen's emerald eyes slid to the next picture, the one that showed the huge dance floor filled with couples.

"I think it's safe to say, you and Xander both did that big white wedding before. So, what's the opposite?" Portia said, closing the album.

"When I was a little girl in County Cork, I always wanted to get married at one of the old, mossy country chapels. Something situated in nature. And something that only has room for the few people that actually matter," Maureen said wistfully, recalling the green and mist.

Portia snapped her fingers. "There's a small, old, Spanish-style chapel on one of the nearby barrier islands."

Nodding, Maureen said, "That could work. Can we check it out?"

Portia shrugged. "As long as we don't take a dip with any alligators, I don't see why not."

Within about fifteen minutes Portia and Maureen had made their way to one of the smaller boats. Portia took up her familiar boat position—clinging to the railing and concentrating on filling her lungs with air. Maureen laughed, admiring her friend's willingness to constantly fling herself into the jaws of anxiety.

The Sunday-afternoon sun stretched long rays in front of them, singeing warmth into Maureen's skin. She drove the boat with a steady hand, anticipation rising as the shoreline of the small barrier island drew closer.

Visible from the shore was a small Spanish chapel. Climbing ivy shrouded the curved façade of the building, with the exception of the wood door. An elaborate bronze cross jutted from the curved roofline. Exotic tropical plants surrounded the chapel, flanking it in natural beauty.

As Maureen anchored the boat, Portia stood on wobbling legs. "What do you think?"

"It's perfect. This is definitely the place." A true smile pushed loose.

"So now that we are here, tell me your vision. I'll help make it tangible."

Maureen blinked, letting her Irish imagination have full rein and dance before her.

"Small. The family and some of the full-time staff for the guest list. Will you be my bridesmaid?" Maureen asked.

"Of course, I will. That's an easy enough request. What else? Colors you have in mind?" Portia pressed, pen to paper.

"Light and natural colors. Orange flowers. They feel like they could have come from this landscape, don't they?"

Portia nodded, scribbling on her legal pad. "Dress?"

Maureen took a moment, letting the image wash over her. "I want Rose to be in a flowing white dress, one with peonies that ripple out of the fabric by her precious feet."

"Gorgeous. What about flowers for her? Perhaps a flower wreath headband?" Portia offered, trying to ride in the direction of Maureen's vision.

Maureen nodded in agreement. "Yes. A beautiful flower crown of orange and white flowers with nice green leaves twined together."

"And how do you envision your dress?"

A pause. Her first wedding dress had been stifling and rigid. The landscape here beckoned for something more natural. "Something strapless. And with ruffles from the waistline down. The kinds of ruffles that look like cascading waves."

"Now *that* I know we can find. And you will look like a fairy-bride in a dress like that. I'll make a few calls to bridal shops as soon as we get back. This is going to be a beautiful ceremony."

Maureen's eyes lingered on the chapel. The echo of a childhood plan rendered real. Or real enough. She could practically picture Rose as the flower girl and Xander, all tall, tan and handsome, standing with her in that chapel.

Tears threatened to blur her vision, a lump pushing in her throat. She knew the wedding would be stunning, and go off without a hitch.

But the wedding night… That was another story. What would it be like after a day of fairy-tale romance? Could she resist Xander when it was just the two of them?

Or, better yet, did she want to?

Eight

Xander slipped on his aviator sunglasses as he stepped outside. Looking for Maureen.

Less than a week until their wedding. Until he could have her. But for now, he'd settle just to see her. Maureen's presence had a steadying effect on him, like a constant drumbeat in a song.

He had a sneaking suspicion of where he'd find her today. His paces eating up the ground fast, he made his way to the wild bird sanctuary and rehab facility. The covered screen area rose high as a palm tree, maybe about twenty feet tall. Maureen worked in the screened area, every bit the sexy wood nymph.

Her hair twisted on her head in a messy ballerina bun, she wiped beads of sweat from her brow. The Florida sun worked overtime, heating the air, turning the midday afternoon sticky with unbridled humidity.

And she still looked damn good.

Xander stood back a moment, drinking her in. She hadn't noticed him yet. He recognized one of the birds from the boat oil spill. The bird seemed to test its wings, stretching them as it perched on her arm.

She cooed at it. Patient. Encouraging. The bird cocked its head at her, as if trying to understand.

"There we go. You've got it." As if in response, the bird bristled its chest, white feathers puffing. But it made no attempt to leave her arm.

"Maybe later, love." She sat the small bird down on a nearby branch. It chirped at her as she turned her attention to an African gray parrot. One with a splinted broken wing. She scrutinized the wing, nose crinkling as she inspected it.

As he approached, Xander noted the way the days out in the sun had left her skin slightly pink. A sunburn, but it colored her fair skin in the appearance of a fixed blush.

Stepping up behind her, he cleared his throat. "Shouldn't you be planning the wedding?"

"We could just go to a justice of the peace."

"We could, but we're looking to make this appear as legit as possible for both our sakes. Need I remind you how high the stakes are for you and for Rose?" The words came out sharply, but damn it, she needed to take this seriously.

Stroking the African gray's feathers, she returned the bird to the low branch.

Casting him a glance over her shoulder, she replied, even-keeled as ever. "You can calm down. Portia and I have everything mapped out. Portia and I already called the caterer and florist this morning. All will be taken care of."

"And your dress?" The dress he wanted to see and then promptly relieve her of.

She chewed her full bottom lip. "I, uh, I'll have one."

"I certainly hope so."

"I have evenings to shop." Her voice wavered and her hands went to her hair, a sign of fraying nerves.

"There are parties planned, you know. As my wife, there will be more functions to attend. It will be good for the refuge, too."

"I understand and I can handle it."

He hooked his arms around her. "Part of this whole deal is appearing like a couple. Starting now."

The heat of her sunburn radiated warmth between them, adding to the electric nature of their embrace. He pulled her closer, bodies practically one. His hand traced up the small of her back, gently outlining her spine, hinting at her generous curves. He wanted her. Not a week from now. But now.

Ever since that night in the hot tub with her, the level of his craving had ratcheted up too high to ignore.

She blinked up at him flirtatiously. "Are you asking to kiss me?"

"Do you want me to?"

Her eyes went sultry. "Well, in the interest of being a good, engaged couple."

He laughed softly. Angling his head to hers, he kissed her. Slowly and thoroughly, long enough to feel her body go limp in his arms. A victory that only made him ache.

Before he lost his senses, he pulled back, away from the fierce temptation her mouth presented. "I have a wedding gift for you."

Her eyes went wide. "You do?"

"Easton and I hired extra help for today so you can have the afternoon and evening off with Portia and your friends here."

"Doing what?" She nibbled her enticing bottom lip, trying to ferret out the information.

He grinned, wishing he could work on that lower lip of hers himself, but he knew that kissing her again would be his undoing. "It's not a gift if it isn't a surprise."

The owner of Je T'aime, Darling passed out five flutes of champagne. Maureen nodded her thanks to the shop owner, wishing it was socially acceptable to down the whole glass before the toast.

Nerves jumbling in her stomach, she surveyed the women that accompanied her as she searched for a picture-perfect dress. Portia sat next to a thin, athletic, brunette woman in a yellow sundress—Allie, one of Maureen's good friends and one of the hardest-working volunteers at the refuge. Jessie, the wife of Don the security guard, reapplied bright pink lipstick before taking the champagne off the tray. Two other volunteers sat on the couch. Maureen's impromptu wedding-dress-shopping gang assembled.

"Now, Portia called ahead and let me know the styles you were interested in. And your size. I've pulled a collection of about five dresses for you to try on. We can add from there." The shopkeeper smiled warmly, pointing to a dressing room. "I'll be standing right in the main area if you need me."

With that the woman turned on her heels, disappearing in a rustle of chiffon behind pale pink curtains.

Maureen smiled at her collection of friends, still apprehensive about picking out a dress.

"To Maureen, the beautiful bride," Allie said, raising her glass.

"To Maureen!" the ladies echoed, full smiles as they raised and clinked their glasses together.

With a practiced, steadied hand, Maureen raised and clinked her glass, slamming the champagne back.

"Well, go on. We want to see you in those gorgeous gowns!" Portia grabbed the empty flute from Maureen, ushering her to the dressing room. "Just remember, we can have anything rush-altered. I've got seamstresses on speed dial."

"Is there anything you don't have covered?" Maureen laughed, slipping into the oversize dressing room. Eyes catching immediately on the floor-length mirror, she noticed how the five gowns were each carefully laid on their own hooks. All waiting for her to try.

"No, not if I can help it." Portia squeezed her hand before returning to the couch with the other ladies.

Maureen gravitated toward the gown in the right corner—a strapless, mermaid-cut ivory dress that had ruching all the way from waist to the floor. She slid out of her blue sundress and into the mermaid gown. Taking a glance in the mirror, she twisted her face in displeasure.

Because this dress pressed the unreal reality of her impending wedding on her? She couldn't tell.

Still, she gathered the dress in her hand, walked out to stand in front of her friends.

"It's a beautiful gown," offered Allie, eyebrows rising as she sipped her champagne.

"But?" Maureen pressed, needing further clarification.

"It hides your pretty curves. So restricting, too. You're like the ocean, love. Movement and passion. You need a dress that shows that exuberance, reflects you," Jessie said, fluffing her blond bob.

Maureen nodded, chewing her lip. She did want a gown that spoke to the vibe of this place she loved so much. The untamed, unstructured grace. "I'll try another."

Back into the dressing room. This time she selected an A-line cut. It, too, was strapless, but a true white. An attendant came out with a series of belts to add to cinch in the waist, starting with a simple braided ribbon. Not right. Then more of a low-lying chain, which wasn't quite right, either.

Then…yes, the attendant placed a wide belt of intricate beads along Maureen's waist, cinching it with ribbons in the back to give the right effect until the band could be fitted and sewed on. From beneath the belt, waves of fabric coalesced, folding in and out like sea water.

She didn't even bother to look at herself in the mirror before striding out to her group. "Well?"

Maureen glanced at her friends on the couch, and then past them, to her reflection in the mirror.

The dress was…

"It's you. Someone stole your spirit and made a dress out of you," Portia breathed, smile widening. All the ladies nodded.

Admiring herself in the mirror, Maureen spun, luxuriating in the swish of fabric, the freedom it promised.

"Can you go tell the shop owner I've made my selection? I don't need to try any more."

"You've got it." Portia stood up from the couch. "And Xander has booked the spa for us. That's up next."

After Maureen changed into her clothes and paid for her dress, the group of ladies found their way back to the limo. The chauffeur set a course for the Oasis Spa, an exclusive resort known for their Swedish massages, kelp-based facials and gel mani-pedi combos. An afternoon of pampering for her and her friends, courtesy of Xander Lourdes.

The limo ride went quickly. Maureen did her best to concentrate, to stay present and calm. But guilt crept into her thoughts. All the levels of deceit gnawed at her ability to enjoy such a kind gesture.

As they entered the marbled room, Maureen's jaw dropped. A water feature trickled down a rock wall, the soft babble of water soothing her along with the scents of lavender and eucalyptus in the air. Calm guitar music melted into the background, layering luxury into the very air. A spread of chocolates, grapes, chocolate-dipped fruits, pastries and cheeses covered a long table. Five plush chairs were arranged in a circle, primed for conversation.

First up, pedicures for the ladies.

"You know, Jessie, I always knew Xander and Maureen would hit it off," Allie said, a sly smile playing on her face.

"Did you, now?" Maureen asked, popping a grape in her mouth.

"Oh, yes. You balance each other. The timing just had to be right. But I saw the spark months ago."

Months ago? He hadn't even been on her radar then. Not in a real way.

"Oh, yes, I can see that, too. He's always had that intense gaze for her, hasn't he?" Jessie agreed, clearly enjoying the pedicure. Her normally tensely furrowed brow seemed to release all tension.

"Ah, yes. And here they are today. Inseparable. In love," Portia added.

A bit *too* quickly, Maureen noted. Wondering, briefly, if she knew the nature of the ruse.

Best not to dwell on that. Instead, Maureen focused on relaxing. Living in the moment, drinking in the layered scents of incense and nail polish. Letting the conversation fall away as her personal attendant shaped her nails.

While their face masks were still setting, her friends told her to close her eyes. More surprises?

"Okay. Open them." Portia urged, placing a shirt in her hand.

Eyes blinking to readjust to the light in the room, she read the shirt. *Bride.* She willed her mouth to smile. "Thank you. It's so kind."

And a lie. But for a minute she wanted it to be true.

"That's not all. We've gotten you something to make your big night and your life together just a little sweeter," Allie said, pulling a perfectly wrapped box out from under her chair.

"Or saucier." A wicked grin escaped Jessie's lips.

Oh, Lord. She was worse than a liar. She was a downright fraud. All of the effort these women had put in on such short notice...

"You all...you all didn't have to do this." Maureen's voice cracked, a hint of shimmering tears beginning to line her eyes.

"Of course, we did. It's not every day you get married. And it's certainly not every day you get married to such a handsome, generous man," Allie chided, unaware that this, in fact, was not Maureen's first jaunt down the aisle. The first wedding had been in earnest and ended in flames. Could a wedding constructed in falsehood somehow fare better? She shoved that thought away.

"Anyway, I want you to open mine first," Jessie said, pushing her silver-wrapped box in front of Maureen. Jessie took a bite of chocolate fudge, motioning Maureen to hurry up.

With shaking fingers, touched and humbled by the attention of these kind woman, she tore through the wrapping paper, lifted the cardboard lid to reveal five smaller boxes, all with little cards affixed to the lids. Each card had a jingle about panties—when to wear each pair. One for the honeymoon. One for their first fight. One for Valentine's Day.

Maureen's face turned upward, light dancing in her eyes. "This is hysterical."

"I thought you'd appreciate them." She winked, biting into a chocolate-covered strawberry.

Maureen unwrapped the rest of the gifts—a few pieces of delicate, lacy lingerie, an embroidered pillow with their names and wedding date, and a tiny, glittering frame.

"Thank you so much. I really appreciate all of this."

"Of course, Maureen. We wanted you to have a special, albeit hastened, bridal shower. Which reminds me. I wrote down all of your reactions to your presents. It's a list I like to call 'Things I Will Say to Xander on Our Wedding Night.'" Portia's smile reached her eyes.

"What?"

"Oh, just listen. 'Things Maureen Will Say to

Xander in Bed.' Ahem. 'This is hysterical. This is so precious! Lord, this is so tiny! Beautiful and delicate. What a pretty shade of pink!'"

Peals of laughter erupted from around the spa room. Her fake bridal shower had been so much more spontaneous and comfortable than her real one. After another two hours of massages, the limo arrived to take them all back to the refuge. Back to Xander. She wanted to thank him for his kindness, to show how much she appreciated him.

She rushed back to her room, slipped into a backless black dress. The front was a deep cowl neck that tastefully nodded to the nature of her curves. Ready to see him. Ready to unwind from the day together.

So eager to see him it almost scared her.

Two hours later, and dinner on the water still made her heart sing. Xander had made reservations at a small, local restaurant. They'd eaten the catch of the day on the deck, watched the sun sink heavy on the horizon and exchanged stories about their childhoods. Gotten to know each other.

The night offered them a degree of comfort—stars dipping in the sky. The lack of true light pollution meant the stars were out in full force, crowning the end of a pretty amazing day. Maureen felt like she lingered on in a fairy world. A slumber that she didn't want to wake from. The whole day had been wonderful. Brilliant.

He helped her into the Mercedes. The touch of his fingertips leaving her wanting. He closed her door, loosened his tie on the way around and climbed into the driver's side. The ride back to the refuge was about five minutes. Too short before they'd part.

Xander parked the Mercedes in the driveway and turned to face her. An eternity passed between them and she stared at his lips, his eyes. He looped his tie around her neck and tugged her toward him. Melting into the feel of him, Maureen inhaled his spicy aftershave, rich with sandalwood and spices and *man*. Greedy with need, their mouths met, parting instantly as they tasted each other for the first time after denying the attraction for so long.

As Xander tunneled his fingers through her hair, it slipped loose, tumbling around them both in a sensuous cloud. Strands spiraling midway along her back tickled down her spine, tingling along her already sensitive skin.

Maureen gripped the lapels of his jacket. Her fingers clenched tight as she strained to get nearer, desperate to deepen the closeness she felt with him, blocking out the rest of the world. Twining her fingers in his hair, she held his face to hers, devouring him, ravenous after what felt like an eternity of waiting. Had this attraction been lurking even longer than she'd allowed herself to acknowledge?

A low groan rumbling in his throat, Xander's leg pressed against hers, the muscles firm, exciting. He covered her body with his, muscled arms lowering her into the corner of the seat. His hand trailed up her leg, stopping to grasp her hip and pull her against him, hard with need.

Maureen arched her back as something uncomfortable prodded her spine. When her body bowed upward, Xander groaned in response and pressed her deeper into the cushioned seat.

"Ouch!" Maureen reached behind her back and tossed a pen case aside.

"Sorry," Xander mumbled against her lips, groping to locate any other possible sharp objects that might distract her. He tossed the pen box over the seat to land in a thudding heap on the floor on top of his briefcase.

"It's okay." Maureen pulled his face back for another mind-drugging kiss.

Xander slipped her dress down one shoulder and cupped her breast, brushing a thumb across the tightened crest, sending sparks of desire through her. When he lowered his mouth to replace his hand, Maureen couldn't control the desire to roll her hips against his. A new music coursed through her as they resumed their dance.

She pushed away any concerns, wanting to revel in him. She'd spent enough time pretending. She wanted something real.

She wanted him.

"Birth control," Xander moaned.

His chest heaving, he rested his head against her breast. Puffy gasps of air dried the damp peak, the painful chill almost as stimulating as his warm, moist kisses.

"You have my mind so muddled I can't think straight half the time." He raked his fingers through his mussed hair. "I can't believe I let things go this far in the driveway, where anyone could walk up on us. Give me a minute to clear my head and figure out where we should go."

Maureen struggled to control the passion singing through her body as she watched Xander, his eyes closed, his breathing ragged. She'd been so determined to wait, but something, maybe the edginess of the storm or the visions of him with his family or just his magnetism altogether, created a different storm inside her and she knew.

She didn't want to wait any longer.

"My place."

"What?"

"Go to my place." Maureen cupped his face in her hands and explained with urgency, "It's private and I have condoms."

His eyes opened wide as realization dawned. "Yes, ma'am."

Rolling off her, Xander turned on the Mercedes and slammed it into gear just as she snapped her seat belt into place. Their labored breathing filled the luxurious car as they made record time through the dirt roads to her cabin. Every stop sign became a sweet temptation as they stole hot, passionate kisses, becoming more familiar with the flavor of each other at every intersection.

After four years of abstinence, she owed it to herself not to wait one minute longer. She stroked up his arm. "Drive faster."

"And you have condoms?"

"An unopened box of a dozen."

"Twelve!" Xander's brow creased into deep fur-
rows while he stared at the road as if pondering a
quadratic equation. "Well, at least that's in the ball-
park if you give me a couple of days. It is a week-
end, after all."

"If only you had one in your wallet."

With a low growl of sexual arousal, he put the
car in Park and reached for her again. "You're driving me crazy."

The second Xander slid to the middle of the front
seat, Maureen straddled his lap. She couldn't remember when sex had been fun. And this was so wonder-
fully abandoned and impulsive, and a huge turn-on.

The skirt of her dress hitched up as she knelt, her
feet dangling off the edge of the seat. She fumbled
with his belt, having difficulty managing even in the
luxury sedan, leather creaking as she moved.

Xander's jaw slid open.

Even though it couldn't go further until they
reached her place, the thick press of his arousal
through his pants pressed against the core of her,
sending sweet sparks of pleasure through her.

Not one to lag behind, he slid his hand under her
dress and skimmed his fingers along the edge of
her panties.

When he gripped her hips, his fingers grazed
across her stomach. She grabbed his wrists and
moved his other hand to cup her breast under the
silky fabric flowing around them both in a fiery
cloud.

Tap-tap-tap.

Maureen flinched.

Xander's head pivoted toward the sound.

Someone with a flashlight strobed the beam in their direction, illuminating Xander's eyes, full of heat and desire. Xander's hands snaked from under her dress with lightning speed.

"Good evening. Is everything okay?" Don, a volunteer, shouted through the window. The older man had worked security detail for a major corporation before retiring, and now volunteered those skills to patrol the refuge at night.

Maureen pressed the electric button, thankful the Mercedes was still running. Easing off Xander's lap, she almost toppled over when he clamped his hands on either side of her dress to hide the considerable evidence of his arousal. The exotic scent of tropical flowers in the night air drifted through the open window as the security guard shuffled his feet.

"Hi, Don. Uh, nice weather." She shifted, sitting on Xander's knees and praying very hard that this nightmare would end—soon.

"Yes, ma'am, mighty nice." Grin spreading across his craggy face, Don thumped his flashlight against his palm, the beam flickering through the dark like a laser show out of control.

"Uh-huh." Maureen unclenched her hands, tight with building desire.

Xander injected into the awkward silence, "How's little Donny Junior?"

"Just fine. He and his wife have a baby on the way."

Maureen felt Xander's glance her way as she focused with undue concentration on the files littering the floor of the car.

Xander cleared his throat. "Tell them I said congratulations."

"Sure will." Don tapped a foot against a tire. "Night, Mr. Lourdes. Good evening, Miz Burke."

She nodded and smiled awkwardly.

Xander waved. "Good night, Don."

With a low chortle, the volunteer security guard turned and strode off into the darkened parking lot.

Maureen raised the window and turned back to Xander just as he adjusted his pants. She clenched the armrest, unsettled by the interruption and by how quickly she'd been swept away by desire for this man.

"Maureen, don't you think you could have helped me out with Don?"

"Nope. I can still barely put two thoughts together." Maureen pressed a hand to her mouth, a hysterical giggle bursting free.

"What?" An indignant expression stained Xander's face as he flopped back against the seat.

"Think about it, Xander."

His shoulders lifted and fell, chuckles rumbling low in his chest. "You make me act like a sixteen-year-old again, making out in a car."

"You must have had a very different life at sixteen than I did. Sorry I didn't consider Don when I, uh, jumped you."

"Don't worry about it. We have a dozen condoms waiting for us at your place."

Nine

From the Mercedes to the cabin door seemed to take an eternity. She stepped in front of him, her slender calves visible in the subdued moonlight, teasing him even more. The promise of her skin against his drove him to madness as she fumbled to slip her keys in the door.

And each step gave him too much damn time to think about the step he was taking—sleeping with a woman for the first time since he'd lost Terri. But she was gone, and he had to move forward with his life. He shut down thoughts of the past that threatened the present.

He wanted this, and Maureen deserved his full attention.

The lock clicked open like a gunshot starting a

marathon race, spurring him to action. They stepped through the frame and he kicked the door closed behind him, kissing her deeply. The soft press of her body against his sent his passion into overdrive.

Her hands wandered over his shirt, undoing each button. Shrugging off the fabric, he broke their embrace. To look at her. To *see* her.

Maureen's wild red hair framed her face, falling just above her breasts. A hunger danced in her green eyes as she stood, pressed against the white wicker sofa in the center of her small living room. The modest cabin was filled with photographs of exotic locales and remnants of her Irish roots in the form of a Celtic Cross centered on the wall behind her. A woman who knew no real borders.

He approached her again, kissing her exposed shoulder, running his hand to the zipper on the back of her satiny dress edged with the gentle rasp of lace. He wanted nothing between them. He couldn't remember when he'd felt so out of control as he'd been in the car. That wasn't his style. He ran the show, called the pace, took things slow and careful. Yet they'd almost forgotten birth control.

Above all, he had to remember to be careful with her, to think of her needs. He didn't want to think about Terri now, but she'd been so delicate. Hell. He shoved thoughts of her aside and focused on this moment and what Maureen wanted. What Maureen needed from him. What he needed from her.

Not that reasonable thought was any easier to find now than in the Mercedes.

She felt exquisitely smooth and soft to his touch. Memories of her bare breasts the day in the hot tub grotto blared into his brain, a vision seared on the backs of his eyelids that he couldn't wait to re-create. Tugging her dress down, down, he unveiled her delicate yellow bra, an expanse of sheer lace with strategic roses stitched to cover the rosy tips.

With a groan, he stripped off the yellow ribbons that served as straps, letting the lace peel down and away. Her back arched, tilting those beautiful breasts toward his mouth. Inviting his kiss. He palmed one creamy weight in his hand, lifting her for a taste.

She hissed a sigh between her teeth, her knees giving way as she fell deeper into him. He anchored her waist with one arm as he rolled one taut nipple between his teeth—gently plucking and licking. Her hair spilled over his arms as she strained to get closer. He molded her waist and hips with his hands, dragging the dress fabric down and off.

Their clothes fell away in a trail on the way to her bedroom, pooling haphazardly on the wood cabin floor.

Entering her bedroom, she pulled out a box of condoms from her driftwood nightstand. They were still sealed. She made no further moves as he joined her near the bed.

He looked at her, questioning. Hoping she still wanted him.

A mischievous look entered her eye. "You can ask."

"Ask what?"

"When I bought them. Why I have them. I bought them after your proposal."

"For this?" He lifted his hand to her face, touching the softness of her wild curls.

She leaned in, kissing the outline of his top lip. "It's been inevitable."

A roar of victory filled his brain as finally, finally, she understood what he'd known in his gut since that impulsive proposal burst from his mouth.

"Nice to hear you acknowledge what I've felt since our first dance together," he said, skimming his lips over hers.

She teased her fingers along his bristly jaw, then back around to the back of his neck, stroking up into his hair. "Because I want you as much as I believe you want me."

Pulling her closer, their bodies pressed together, he reveled in the brush of their bare flesh against flesh, their legs tangling. One hand between her shoulder blades, his other against her spine, he lowered her onto the thick duvet and covered her body with his. The mattress gave beneath them, her curves molding to his, sending his need into intense overdrive.

The ceiling fan stirred gusts of air over their rapidly heating flesh as his hands learned the terrain of her every curve. As she reciprocated. It was so natural. So right.

And so well lit, thanks to the bedside lamp.

He couldn't have dreamed anything more perfect. And he wasn't sure how much longer he could wait.

Just when he thought he'd reached the breaking point, he saw her pat the bed for the box of condoms and, yes, he was more than happy to assist. Quickly.

At the last instant she snatched a packet from his hands and tore it open. Maureen sheathed the throbbing length of him with deliberate—oh, so deliberate—control. Slowly. Almost torturously slowly, and her smile said she understood well how close she danced to the very hot flame of desire.

His hands tangled in her hair, he kissed her, thoroughly, sealing their lips, their tongues mating as he pushed inside her body for the first time. Felt the hot clamp of her around him, drawing him in, welcoming him.

Bringing him such intense pleasure he almost flew over the edge right then and there.

But he held on, holding still until he had enough self-control to move again, with her, in and out, thrusting and guiding her hips with the rock of his against hers. He took each kittenish gasp of pleasure into his mouth, grazing kisses along her jaw, then her neck as her head flung back, exposing the graceful arch. Her riotous red hair splayed over the pillow like a fire he would never forget. Ever.

She pushed against his shoulders, rolling him to his back, her magnificent hair draping forward in long, tangled curls over her shoulders, skimming the tops of her breasts. His hands slid from her hips up to cup the weight of her, his thumbs grazing her until her nipples tightened into peaks of pleasure.

The *hmm* of bliss rolling up her throat and between her lips encouraged him as much as the roll of her hips as she rode him, drawing out the pleasure between them.

He pulled her closer to him, needing to feel the curve of soft breasts in his palms. Leaning forward, she kissed his neck, breath heavy and urgent. Hand slipping on her back, pushing her farther. Needing more of her.

He gritted his teeth to hold back the urge to come. Now. Hard and fast. But he wasn't finishing without her. He was determined to see the ecstasy of release stamped on her face, flushing her bare flesh.

Audible moans rose from her, encouraging him to hold on longer. The long red curls that shadowed her face a moment ago flipped back. She arched in pleasure as her body throbbed around him with ripples of her orgasm, massaging him into a release that sent his head pressing back into the pillow.

Then in a flash, he rolled her to her back again and thrust once, twice more, drawing an additional moan of pleasure from her.

He sighed deeply, pulling her to his chest. No words, just the sound of labored breathing growing calm. Her leg snaked around his, breasts and thighs against his side.

She mumbled against him, kissing his shoulder. "That was…perfect."

He skimmed his mouth along the top of her head. "Damn straight it was and the next time will be even better if possible. I have plans for you, lady."

"Hmm—" she hummed against him "—I like the sound of that…" Her voice trailed off.

"Maureen?"

"Yes," she said in a whisper.

"Are you with me?"

"Uh-huh," she murmured. "Just deliciously mellow and recharging for the next…round…"

Maureen's breath slowed more, sleep finding her.

Sweat trickled on his brow, cooling him physically.

Emotionally? He revved up thinking of the next time he'd have her once she woke. For now, though, he couldn't help but be glad for the chance to get his thoughts together. Because his world had just been rocked. He hadn't felt this way in a damn long time.

Not since Terri. He hadn't had sex since his wife had passed away. Fourteen months and it all had come down to this moment. A moment he had angled for. Wanted. And, more importantly, *enjoyed*.

But that didn't change the fact that conflict swirled like a burgeoning hurricane in his heart. Maureen rolled slightly away from him, the sudden space between their bodies sending a brief chill through him. Already aching over that absence, he knew his feelings for Maureen had transitioned. Not tonight, exactly. He couldn't tell when it had happened.

Xander was starting to experience more than just lust for her. Something so much more. Something that scared the hell out of him. He felt disloyal to the memory of Terri as he lay in bed, tangled with Maureen.

And for Maureen. Would this complicate how she approached their marriage of convenience?

His thoughts picked up force, that familiar tightness in his gut howling.

Distance and space. He needed that now. Needed to sort all of this out. Carefully, Xander pulled his arm out from beneath Maureen. She stirred but didn't wake. Even sleeping, her expression seemed kind.

The last thing he wanted to do was hurt her. Gathering up his clothes, he dressed. Taking one last look at her, he noted the way the covers dipped with her hourglass figure. His eyes slid to the box of condoms. Eleven left. Part of him wished he could have used more tonight. He wished a lot of things and had damn few answers to his questions.

Dressing the next morning, Maureen told herself she wasn't upset Xander hadn't been in bed when she'd woken. That was fine. Really.

She'd curled up beside him again and drifted often, expecting a morning of leisurely wake-up sex. And instead found a cold pillow that still carried a hint of dampness from his showered hair.

Maureen went through a rational list of reasons why he'd left before she woke up. He did have a child. And with his in-laws breathing down his neck, he probably needed to make sure he didn't appear negligent or selfish. That explanation seemed satisfactory.

Besides, even though she and Xander were technically engaged, his early morning departure effectively eradicated the possibility of too much gossip around the refuge. Another aspect she greatly appreciated. Appearing engaged and in love was one thing. Having people watching him slip out of her cabin and fill in lurid details was another altogether. This was all still so new to her.

She refused to let her mind wander to more sinister reasons. There'd be no good in that.

Over the past few days he'd been so kind to her. Filled her hours with surprises—the spa day with her friends, dinner. Maureen desperately wanted to do something for him. So he'd know how much she appreciated his gestures and actions. Before this all fizzled away and she was forced back to reality with only a couple of days left until the wedding.

Her wedding, the reality that she would really be staying in the States, reminded her of her home in Ireland and all of the things she'd left behind. She was committed to staying here, wanted to stay in the States, but daily she'd had to remind herself that might not be possible. It still might not be possible for any number of reasons if—when—she and Xander split. If she were to survive that transition, she wanted to make sure she and Xander parted as good friends. Maureen needed to build her fake marriage on something real.

She and her ex were like an arsonist and a lit match. While the flaming love sounded poetic, its reality manifested in destruction. Damaging. The ashes of that life still swirled around her.

After her fake marriage ended, she didn't want to

find herself again in a burn pit of ruins. *After*. The reality of *after* bit at her, nipped at her mind.

What did she want after? To really return to Ireland? To leave Xander and Rose? The refuge?

So many pounding questions she couldn't deal with. Instead, she dressed in coral-colored shorts and a flowing white top, and went to pick up pastries for Xander. A small surprise, but food always had a way of easing tension between people.

Knocking on the door to the main house, pastries in hand, Maureen's thoughts entered the now-familiar circle in her mind. Xander. What did he do for fun? He didn't appear to have any hobbies. His interests seemed to be work and caring for Rose.

Part of her wondered if he didn't allow himself any quiet time. Time when he'd have to face realities he seemed desperate to escape. Or maybe that was just her. She'd always pushed into work in moments of stress and uncertainty. Maybe he did the same.

The door swung open, interrupting her thoughts. The afternoon sun soaked into Xander's cool blue eyes and tanned skin. Sexy still. Her belly did a little backflip, nerves prickling her face into a smile.

"I brought pastries." She extended the box to him.

"You'll be bringing those to go. I was actually headed to come surprise you. I've got a whole afternoon and evening planned for us. And Rose." There was a lightness in his voice that didn't fully reach his eyes.

Maureen blamed it on the strength of the sun, taking the gesture of an impromptu date more seriously than the lack of sparkle in those eyes. She tried to guess the nature of the date from his clothes: khaki shorts, a polo shirt that matched his eyes and leather boat shoes that finished off his casual look so different from his office suits and formal tuxedos.

He'd been prepared for her. Within five minutes, the little trio packed into the limo. The nanny had already left ahead of them to set things up in the hotel. Rose chattered in her car seat, grabbing for Maureen's hair. They set out for a tiny neighboring island where a street market filled with entertainment and life flourished like a school of vibrant fish.

Maureen carried Rose on her hip, relishing the smile on the baby's face. She liked the way Rose drank in the scenery, cooed at the street musicians. So aware for one so young. A natural-born observer, perhaps a future scientist in the making.

"Xander, last night was…beautiful," Maureen said softly, her gaze focused away from him, "but I can't help wondering why you didn't say goodbye."

He paused for an instant before answering. "I didn't want to wake you."

"Hmm," she said softly. "That sounds a bit like a cop-out to me."

His shoes thudded along the boardwalk. "You're a smart woman. So, okay, I'll be honest. It was the first time I've been with anyone since Terri died and I needed to gather my thoughts."

She glanced up at him. "It was a first for me, too, since my divorce. That takes a lot of trust on both of our parts, I'm thinking."

He nodded. "I believe you're right."

Silence fell between them again, more comfortable in some ways but also more intense as they both openly acknowledged the shift in their relationship. This wasn't just about Rose or paperwork or interfering in-laws anymore.

Xander stroked Maureen's back as they walked. For a few brief, shining hours she felt a sense of togetherness. Like they were a real couple, a real family. Like she'd actually gained entrance into this world. That there wasn't a fake marriage tied to her pear-shaped ring that glittered in the fading light.

They paused on the brick-paved street. Maureen leaned into Xander. Wrapping his arm around her shoulder, they watched a street performer juggle a pineapple and a sword. The action made Maureen a little queasy, but the juggler moved with a dancer's grace. A small, collapsible black table stood in front of him. With breakneck speed, the juggler tossed the pineapple to the table, grabbed the sword by the hilt and sliced open the fruit.

"Impressive," Xander murmured right as Rose began to cry hysterically. Maureen's maternal instincts stimulated, she began to rock Rose, speaking in a soothing voice.

To no avail.

Glancing at his bronze-faced watch, Xander cleared his throat. "I think she's exhausted. It's a little past her bedtime. Come on, let's go to the Dolphin's Tale and meet the nanny. She'll put her down and we'll have time alone. Just you and me. No more talk or interference of the past."

The promise of his words struck a chord in her, reassuring her.

They walked down the street, to the quaint but well-appointed bed-and-breakfast. The dying light sinking into the ocean seemed to absorb the fair pink color of the building, making it part of the sunset. Elenora was waiting in the lobby for them.

"Shall we?" Xander extended his arm to Maureen. She grabbed it, nodding. "I hope you don't scare easy." A laugh rolled off his tongue like a stray wave on a calm day.

"Why?" She squeezed his arm, having enjoyed the day more than she possibly could have imagined a couple of weeks ago.

Not that she would have imagined any of this two weeks ago. Could it be real so fast? Or was it as simple as the plan he'd stated at the outset?

Old insecurities were difficult to shake.

"You'll see." He maneuvered them toward a party boat designed to hold a couple dozen tourists, the craft moored at a nearby dock.

They boarded the boat and the guide began telling legends of ghosts and vampires. Tracking over to a smaller island's shore, the tour group followed the guide on the sand, huddled close to hear about gruesome deaths and hauntings that chilled Maureen, making her hold tighter to Xander.

"What made you think of this?" Maureen asked

on the way back to the main island, wind causing her hair to have a life of its own.

He shrugged, looking at the water below the railing. "I tried to imagine the date a scientist would have never considered."

"Vampires. Good guess."

"So you've never been to Transylvania." He laughed but his gaze seemed to travel past her.

What was he thinking? Were his thoughts drifting back to his dead wife in spite of what he'd said earlier?

"Can't say that I have. I still remember coming to the States as a child and realizing how the size of everything is…overwhelming. But in an amazing way. I love my home country and I miss so much about it, but the space here, the expanses and vast differences in terrain that offer so much for my mind to ponder… I feel at home here, as well. It wasn't hard to run here when I needed to leave."

"God, Maureen…" Night wind tore at his jet-black hair. "I'm sorry taking the job on Key Largo happened under duress." His answer seemed more rote than governed by feeling. This couldn't all be in her head. Something was definitely off.

"I don't want to talk about that. I love my job. I love being here. And we had an amazing night out." She tried to shift the focus back to the positive. Putting them back into the moment of this lovely night. They both seemed to need that.

"Okay," he said, turning to her, the light entering his eyes again as he rejoined the lighter mood she'd sought, "so no Transylvania trip as a kid. What about vampire crushes as a teenager?"

She smiled, toying with the button on his polo shirt. "What teenage girl hasn't read some kind of vampire hot-hero story and imagined being in love forever?"

"That's the appeal? The forever part?" He guided her onto an empty bench seat, shrouded in a bit of darkness and privacy from the other passengers.

"And the sexy charisma. The machismo. You have that—without the fangs."

"I can still bite. Lightly, of course, and in just the right places." He kissed her neck, playfully nipping it.

She shivered. "You're bad."

"I thought I was a starched-shirt businessman."

"You're a…surprise."

"That's good. I used to wonder why you and my brother didn't end up together." Was this why he was distant? Fear of a crush on his free-spirited younger brother? That kind of fear she could squash.

"Three reasons."

"Care to share?"

She sipped the bottle of water the guide had distributed earlier in the evening. "We're too much alike. There's no chemistry. And I think he has a thing for Portia."

"Portia? For real? They can barely stand working together. I've never even been sure why he keeps her on the payroll other than the fact most people wouldn't put up with him. I'm even more bemused as to why she stays."

She cast him a sidelong glance as the boat drew closer to the dock. Could he really be that oblivious? "And that should tell you something."

"Good point."

Leaning against the rail, she inspected her leather bracelet as the boat pulled up to the dock. The boat came to an abrupt stop, causing Xander to press against her slightly.

"I'm not sure and, certainly, I've never seen anything concrete. It's just an impression I get sometimes," she said as the crew finished tying off the boat and placing the debarking plank so the passengers could leave.

They made their way to the exit, falling into line with the others in the group.

"You have good instincts. That's clear." He helped her down off the boat ramp, his grip light and loose.

"Thank you. That's a lovely thing to say." While he hadn't stopped touching her all night, she could hear the distance in his voice.

"It's just the truth." Grasping her hand, they meandered on the sidewalk. Bars filled with loud, live music jumbled together. Their discordant mingling reminding Maureen of the play she'd studied while at university—*The Rites of Spring*. The disorientation extended beyond the framing of the various bands' sounds. She didn't know how to ease whatever troubled Xander.

"Still, thank you for the compliment."

"You deserve it and so many more. You're an incredibly resilient, compassionate and accomplished woman—which all makes you even hotter than you already are, which is mighty damn hot."

Playfully shoving him away, she stopped on the corner before the Dolphin's Tale, eyebrows raised incredulously, more than a little concerned. A horribly failed marriage could do that to a person. "Are you for real or playing me?"

"I hope you know me well enough to realize I shoot straight from the hip. I always have. Dishonesty in business and life gets you nowhere fast." He closed the distance, grabbing her hand. His intense eyes fixed on her, undoing her doubts slightly. This was the most honest he'd been all day. She could tell he meant it.

"I have to agree. Honesty is crucial. Dishonesty always comes back around. Karma's a bitch."

"A bitch with vampire fangs." He gave her a long, sensual look of promise.

This evening's date had clearly brought up more questions than answers, leaving her more confused and unsure than ever. She should be content. All would be well when it came to enjoying their short-term marriage of convenience.

She twisted the ring on her finger and wondered at the odd squeeze of her heart that warned her she could be getting in over her head.

Leading her up the wooden stairs of the Dolphin's Tale, he noticed a shift in Maureen's demeanor. She seemed subdued. A far cry from the siren in the pool the other night. Or from the woman he'd taken to bed last night and, damn it, that was his fault—for bailing on her after their night of sex. He'd let his own mixed emotions about making love for the first time after Terri's death lead him to disregard Maureen's feelings.

Unforgivable.

Thoughtfully, he opened the pale yellow door, stepping into the main lobby of the bed-and-breakfast. Tasteful experimental coastal art framed the room; it had a lot in common with an art gallery showroom. The harpist played in the back corner, her fingers nimbly plucking an old crooner's song about paper moons and love.

Placing his hand on the small of her back, he led her to their room, sending her inside. Stepping up to the bamboo drink cart, he opened the bottle of chardonnay, pouring Maureen a glass. She lingered a few feet away, absently placing her soft brown purse on the glass living room table. Leaning against the overstuffed couch, she stared into the bedroom off to the left. The plush mahogany four-poster was framed in billowing white tufts of sheer fabric. An inviting space.

He laughed softly. "I brought my own this time."

She turned on her heel and looked at him through her eyelashes. "I like a man who thinks ahead. Impulsive is nice, too."

"I can do that. Think fast on my feet. But keep in mind I'm the analytical type, the kind who has a very distinct plan to bring you complete and utter bliss. Soon. Very soon."

Her lips parted, driving him wild. "I'll be right back. Don't go anywhere," he replied huskily.

Slipping from the room, he checked on Rose and the nanny before rejoining her. Elenora reported Rose had fussed, but slept soundly now. On her way out of the room, the nanny handed over the baby monitor. He smiled, ready to return to Maureen.

Pausing outside the door, he thought about where this—all of this—was heading. He could sense that Maureen felt how he'd coiled like a pygmy rattler today. Xander's retreat had had little to do with her, though. Mostly, his distance had been from a lifetime of too many endings and partings.

Hand on the decadent crystal doorknob, he focused fully on this moment. This woman.

He needed more than just sex from her and a business deal. He needed the oblivion being with her could bring. A tangible, incredible connection between them. Something to stand on. Her caring heart, her banter. Maureen's empathy made him want to be better. Opening the door, he smiled at her. Ready to try harder than before. Feeling as light as the breeze that drifted in from the window overlooking a blackened sea and dew-dripped stars.

When he returned, she stood, sipping the glass of wine he'd poured for her, lingering at the threshold of the bedroom. He approached her, eager as ever. He took the wineglass, set it aside and eased her back on the bed, her legs draped off as he skimmed her dress up.

She laughed softly. "The wicked man is back."

"Do you want to talk?" He nuzzled the inside of her thigh. "Or do you want to see just how bad I can be?"

He snapped the edge of her panties.

"Talking finished," she said succinctly just as he nuzzled between her legs.

He swept off her satin underwear and found the core of her, inhaling her feminine scent of jasmine and desire. With a flick of his tongue, he heard her moan, caught a glimpse of her twisting her hands in the covers. He continued to push her, feeling her hips pulse up to him beneath his tongue. Her breath growing more clipped, more hitched. His own desire ramping up—

Only to be interrupted by the nursery monitor shrieking to life. A deep wail blared through, followed by another. And another, each more urgent than before.

Ten

Rose's wails tore at Maureen's ears, spurring her limbs to move. Xander snapped back, gaze flying to the baby monitor and then to Maureen. He pulled on sweats and a T-shirt as she yanked her panties on, trailing after Xander out of the bedroom, heading for the door. As she passed the couch, she grabbed a robe, feeling the need for more coverage, but she didn't break stride.

The urge to make sure Rose was okay flooded Maureen's awareness. Popping open the door to the baby's room, Maureen tightened the robe's tie. From the corner of her eye, Maureen noticed Elenora's sleep-bleary face emerge from the bedroom as the woman headed for the crib.

Maureen's gait broke into a near-run, needing to

check on Rose herself. Lifting Rose out of the crib, a relief washed through her.

Elenora extended her arms. "I'm sorry she disturbed you both. I can take her."

Maureen shook her head. "I've got her. Truly, no worries. It's okay, Rose, sweetie." Lifting the toddler to her shoulder, she patted her back. Maureen had never spent much time around babies, but there seemed to be a natural maternal instinct she must have tapped into.

Elenora stepped away, waiting in the shadows.

From a distance, Maureen had watched Rose grow up. She'd known Rose for the baby's entire life. But over the last few days, and especially tonight, a chord had been struck. A shift, perhaps, as she realized the larger role she would be playing in this little girl's life. One that represented every complicated aspect of her relationship to Xander.

Maureen would be moving into the house, living with Rose, would become her stepmother. And inhaling the baby shampoo scent, feeling that soft little cheek against hers, Maureen realized that stepping back when the marriage ended was going to be far more complicated than she'd considered in the mad rush to the altar as a way to solve their immediate problems.

Nevertheless, a new feeling of closeness, affection, love for this little life twisted in her heart. She made *shush-shush-shushing* noises as she rubbed soothing circles on Rose's back, the cotton footie pajamas soft against her palm.

Xander walked up behind Maureen. She could feel the heat of him before she heard him, felt his hand on her shoulder.

"Is Rose okay?"

Maureen felt the baby's soft, plump cheek. Turning to face him. "She doesn't feel feverish. Maybe just a baby dream or gas pain?"

Elenora, reaching for Rose, added gently, "I can take her now."

Maureen glanced at Xander and saw the answer in his eyes, an answer that mirrored her own instinct. "We're going to stay with her until she falls back asleep, and then we'll keep the monitor with us. Please, you go ahead and rest."

Xander slid his arm along Maureen's waist. "Yes, please, rest. We'll need your help with Rose tomorrow since we'll be busy with company and finalizing wedding plans."

Maureen's stomach fluttered. Wedding finalization? Only two days left until they exchanged vows. Until their lives were tied. Until this little girl would be her stepdaughter.

And Xander would be her husband. At least temporarily.

Back home again the next day, Xander sat on a beached piece of palm that had probably floated in with the storm. Elbows on his knees, his blue eyes scanned the lapping turf in front of him. A few gulls added their sounds to the rhythm of waves and the soft laughter of Rose.

The objective of the early afternoon? Wear Rose out so she napped soundly since she'd snagged a catnap on the trip home this morning. That would free up some time to finalize wedding details with Maureen.

Wedding details.

As he thought about the ceremony only two days away, his heart tightened. He hoped Maureen felt welcomed and like a part of his small, fractured family. He wasn't sure why it was so important, but he needed her to. Even as he still grieved over the loss of Terri—he would always love her—he knew he had to do this. Hell, he wanted to. Maureen was a good fit in his life. She'd helped him wake up again. This was good for him and for Rose.

So far, his in-laws had made it clear they wanted no part of seeing their son-in-law get remarried. And while he was sad they felt that way, at least the decision was made. He hoped over time they could have a more amicable relationship and accept Maureen.

A vision filled his head of how at ease she was with his child. When they'd spent the night at the bed-and-breakfast, Maureen had sprung for Rose with feline grace and a mother's power. A natural-born nurturer.

A fact Xander had always understood about her, but in that moment he'd seen how deep that inner chord vibrated.

Even now, on the beach, he watched Rose's easy smile. A trusting one. Her shining eyes on Maureen's delicate face. No doubt about it. A bond had been forged between the two of them.

Maureen sat crouched in the shallow crystalline water of a recently developed tide pool. She splashed the cool water on Rose's legs as unadulterated laughter erupted from his daughter's lips.

The scene seemed perfect. Downright natural. He scraped sand between his toes, understanding gathering in his mind as a gust of wind knocked into his chest, the salt heavy on the air and the faint spray of water finding his cheek.

When Maureen left…

Lord. The thought scared the hell out of him. No, she wasn't Terri. He knew that. But Maureen was a woman who deeply cared for Rose. Showed her love and support. Bonded with Rose.

And when she left after the end of this fake marriage? What would happen to Rose?

Devastation.

He knew the feeling. Even though his own mother had left him in his later years, he understood what kind of vacuum that created. A damn hole that billowed open, the result of trusting in a vanishing act.

Maureen caught his gaze, a smile gracing her fair skin, tugging all the way up to her eyes. She began to sing an old Irish song to Rose. In her pink-and-white swimsuit, Rose clapped her hands together, enjoying the sound of Maureen's soft voice.

Damn. That gaze. That heart. He didn't want to lose that. They'd begun to forge a real friendship and their banter made him feel alive. He didn't want to lose that, either.

No, he had to find a way to convince her to stay. And not just for a year. Or even five.

Maybe forever? Something he damn well should start thinking about. The thought gave him qualms, no question, because the thought of having her around permanently sounded good. Too good. It was getting harder and harder to convince himself he was just doing this for Rose.

Xander leaped from log to shore, going to join the ladies who held his heart captive.

Checking her watch, Maureen looked at him. "Time for Rose to nap already?" Her eyes scrunched, squinting in the sunlight.

"It appears that way. I'll carry her." Xander hoisted Rose into his arms. But she grabbed for Maureen.

"I've got her," she said, glowing slightly. "I'll put her down, and I'll be back soon." Taking Rose on her hip, she squeezed his hand, that familiar electricity pulsing in her gaze. Dropping both his hand and gaze, she made her way back to the main house.

Xander put a palm to the back of his neck, massaging it gently as he watched her walk away.

A low whistle sounded behind him. Easton. He'd forgotten his brother was coming to meet him to go over his best-man duties.

"Dive, shall we?" Easton said with a theatrical wave of his hand, alluding to the water in front of him. He had two sets of gear slung over his back.

A dive would probably clear his head. "Done."

They suited up, pushing into the crystal water, heading to the reef.

Once submerged, Xander did his best to feel present, notice the parrot fish, the flow of the anemones and smaller tropical sea creatures. The reef looked like the home of a mermaid queen—and that brought his mind straight back to Maureen.

He motioned to Easton to go back up to the surface. Xander loved the way the sun looked like stained glass from beneath the water and how, since he was a kid, breaking the surface always made him feel like he busted through glass.

Once they both reached the surface, they began treading water, removing the gear so they could talk.

"Know what I love?" Easton said, voice cutting into the air.

"A good, adrenaline-filled vacation?"

Easton's lips curled into a smile. "Well that, obviously, but that I'm a best man twice to my big brother. Seriously. How are you doing and what do you need from me?"

How was he doing? What a loaded question. Xander stayed quiet for a moment, considering how to answer.

In the pause, Easton continued. "The flavor of the speech would be a good place to start."

"Oh, well, nothing that will turn my bride scarlet. Or me, for that matter."

"So I shouldn't mention the run-in with Don the security guy?" Easton winked, devilish mischief in his eyes. Xander stared at him, laughing slightly. "I'm kidding and you know it. My toast will be funny but tasteful. Just like last time."

"But this isn't like last time." Xander breathed, arms moving through the water with more determination than before.

"I know it's not. Mom's not going to be there this time."

Xander had known this, but the reaffirmation of her absence cut still. "Do you think she'll ever stay in one place?"

"Mom is the actual embodiment of wanderlust. I know we all traveled a lot, but I get the feeling Dad had reined in Mom's tendency for that vagabond life." Easton tilted his head, started heading for the shore.

"Yeah. I think you are right. He balanced her out. Grounded her." Xander kicked his feet beneath the water, gaining forward motion, slinging seaweed.

"Listen, I know I accused you of just being in lust the other week...but something seems to have shifted with you two."

"Something has. I think." But was it enough? The women in his life wandered in and out of his story so easily. Too easily. Terri. His mother.

He wouldn't add Maureen's name to that list.

The ground buzzed with movement. Volunteers with flowers, tables and chairs flooded the grounds, transforming the great yard of the refuge into a beautiful rehearsal dinner area.

Maureen sat perched on the edge of an oversize wood chair on the main house's balcony. Watching her fairy-tale wedding come together. And it was a fairy-tale wedding, wasn't it?

She had to keep reminding herself this was scripted, fictional, fabricated. Her heart could not take any more abuse or ache. Still, she couldn't stop the rush of attraction—and more—that caught her unaware every time he walked in the room.

Even when his name was mentioned. She was completely and totally infatuated with this man. She liked him, respected him. Found her daydreams drifting to thoughts of him and plans for ways they could spend time together, ways to help him find more fun in life so she could see that smile spread across his handsome face.

She caught sight of Portia and Easton directing the catering company around. They'd be up here soon, to finalize details. To make sure the whole event went off without a hitch.

Xander set down his tall glass of lemonade on the table, calling her back to their plans.

The honeymoon.

"So, we've narrowed it between Greece and Sicily. But, my Irish lass, I want you to have the final say." He grabbed her hand, stroking his thumb over hers.

The warmth of his gentle touch made her belly flip. She kept thinking she would get used to this— the incredible way he made her feel every time he put his hands on her. But, if anything, each time they were together amped up her attraction. Tilted her whole world on its axis until she seemed to always lean toward him.

"So much pressure, sir."

He looked at her sidelong. "You can handle it."

She chewed her lip, looking at the two vacation itineraries before her, both of which would start with a night in a local cabana before a flight somewhere romantic the day after the wedding. "Sicily."

"That's what I was going to pick, too." He raised her hand to his lips, kissed it gently, sending sparks through her.

Still holding on to her, he looked at her, blue eyes as soft and clear as summer. "Have you ever thought about having children of your own?"

The question became a harpoon lodging in her chest, and she let herself collect her breath by glancing at the wedding preparations: a floral arch being delivered, exotic blooms unloaded in sprays from a truck, and the food van—so much food.

Finally, she turned back to Xander to answer his question, which had caught her so unaware. "Of course I've thought about it. But after my divorce I realized my work is my family. The animals I save and work with are, in effect, my children."

"But you could still have a baby, too."

She shook her head. "I'm not marrying again." Her heart couldn't allow it.

"You already have." Xander gestured to the bustle below.

"I meant after we finish our arrangement."

His dark eyebrows knotted, a storm descending

on his face. Shifting to a serious tone, he leaned forward. "But this—as you call it—*arrangement* is going well. We get along. We're compatible in bed and out. You're fantastic with Rose. We could build a family."

Build a family? A fake family?

She wanted him. Cared for him and Rose. But to be with a man who didn't love her. And to be with a man who wouldn't ever love her? She couldn't do that. Couldn't break again like that.

"You're backing out of our agreement."

He blinked at her. "What?"

"You're scared of losing Rose so you're trying to bribe me into staying longer." That had to be what this was about. No other explanation seemed logical.

"Damn it, no. You've misunderstood my meaning altogether. I was being honest. I think we could build a great life together."

Her Irish temper surged, a storm of her own infusing her voice with anger. And pain. "And so you're offering me a baby if I stay?"

"You're twisting everything I'm saying. We're going to be married. Why not stay that way? You said you're not waiting for another man. So let's share our lives. Be friends."

"Friends?" The last time she checked, marriage was about more than friendship. *Love.* There had to be love, too.

"With benefits and a ring, and a family and common interests. It's actually a stronger foundation than most marriages out there. Think about it tonight."

So, the stiff-shirt businessman returned. The engagement and marriage had been calculated. Sure. But this? A whole new level.

He leaned in to kiss her. But feeling deceived, she angled away under the excuse of conferring with the florist, wondering if she could really go through with this, after all.

The next morning Xander stood outside Maureen's cabin, rolling the simple gold band between his fingers. Maybe it was bad luck to see the bride before the wedding, but he needed to look into her eyes before they said their vows. While he didn't expect the unrestrained joy of his first wedding, things still felt too unsettled.

He'd been trying to reconcile his feelings for Terri, a love he feared he might never know again. But then, too, he was afraid to let what he felt for Maureen really flourish since it seemed like he would be robbing his first marriage of the bond he'd always felt for Terri and he didn't want to let go of that for Rose's sake.

After their seaside argument, Xander had wanted to run for the hills and stay a single man forever, parent his child and hire the best damn lawyers possible to reach an amenable arrangement for his in-laws to safely visit their granddaughter. He would live a satisfying life watching his daughter grow up, work the hours he wanted and watch football games on a wide screen TV with his brother.

Later that night, Xander had thought through his

options as he lay in bed staring at the ceiling, missing Maureen. Though a calculating businessman, his rationale for wanting Maureen to stay had little to do with logic. But to persuade her, he needed to present it in a way that made practical sense. Rose grew more and more attached to Maureen by the day. To rip her away from Maureen would completely fracture Rose's young life.

And, damn it, he wanted Maureen in his life, too. He couldn't deny that. They had a solid friendship. Chemistry. A mutual desire to stay here. Tons of things in common. She was the one he wanted to vent to and laugh with. He'd become quite fond of the way her nose crinkled, and her fiery spirit. That didn't diminish his love for Terri. The women were different. Comparing would be unfair to both of them.

Standing outside Maureen's cabin on their wedding day, with the sun beaming in a cloudless sky, he still couldn't decide what it was about her that entranced him beyond the normal realm of sexual attraction. She wasn't at all his type. Yet when they were together, he felt alive, happy…in a way he hadn't in a long time.

In the midst of all the confusion, one thought remained clear to Xander. He wanted Maureen. He wouldn't let it take anything from his marriage with Terri, but he would enjoy being with Maureen.

Xander tucked the ring into the inside pocket of his charcoal-gray suit coat. He rang the bell and stepped back, leaning against a porch post.

Maureen answered, half dressed. She wore a pale

blue satin gown, her makeup soft and natural, accenting her Irish eyes. Everything about her glowed, Xander thought, as his gaze swept down.

Even her nail polish shimmered.

Looking more than a little nervous, Maureen wiggled her toes, emphasizing that sparkly pedicure. "You caught me before I had a chance to finish dressing. Portia and Jessie are inside. Don't let them catch you."

Relaxing into the safety shield of banter, Xander resumed his lazy position against the post and gestured with a small nod of his head. "Come here and they won't, lady."

Maureen smiled stiffly, unsettled by his words. "Who me?"

"Yeah, you."

She padded across the porch, stopping just in front of him. A breeze blew the skirt of her dress across his legs. The scent of her shampoo and her jasmine perfume teased his senses.

He skimmed his knuckles across her velvety cheek. "Do you mind if I muss you up a bit?"

"Please." Her arms rested by her sides as she pressed her full length to his.

Xander slipped one hand behind her head and cupped her neck. With the other, he palmed her waist, his hand tightening instinctively as the feel of her tingled up his arm. Maureen slid her hand inside his jacket, her fingers spreading wide against his chest, digging past his shirt, imprinting his skin.

He guided her face to his, pressing his lips to

hers, flicking his tongue along the seam of her full mouth. She opened, begging for more, needing the reassurance of connecting on any level they could find after their tense, uncertain time apart. With a gentle moan, Maureen slid her arms around Xander's neck, deepening their kiss. Their mouths mated with the familiar yet unexplainable frenzy both had come to accept as inevitable.

And in less than two hours they would be married. For better.

Or worse?

Eleven

In the end, Maureen ditched her shoes just before entering the chapel, wanting instead to make her vows in the ruins of the old church with the soles of her feet pressing into the cool stone slab of the floor. She needed to ground herself in reality, even if only through the sense of the ground beneath her feet.

This wasn't a real wedding.

They were entering this union for practical reasons only.

She couldn't afford to forget that. Her heart couldn't take another round of marital rejection.

Nerves dancing in her stomach, she held her small bouquet of white peonies as a trio of guitarists began playing, their stringed music filling the space with a harp-like quality that carried a hint of local flair. Perfect.

Except, was it really?

Her mind floated back to a letter she'd been terrified to read but had read anyway. Moments before the ceremony—a choice she regretted now. A wildlife refuge in Killarney had offered her a job.

A job in her home country. She'd applied when she'd thought the expiration of her work visa was inevitable.

She didn't even want the job. Not really. But knowing she had this option—a plan of her own that could have been in play—knotted her gut with tension and fear and the realization of how high today's stakes were. How important it was to make the right choice.

Her growing feelings for Xander made her feel out of control. Filled with an urgency to flee.

But she knew better. She had to go through with this for so many reasons, not the least of which being that she couldn't let Xander and Rose down.

Portia stood just ahead of her, ready to do her maid of honor walk down the aisle with baby Rose on her hip. Before they began the trek to the altar, Maureen leaned down to kiss Rose's cheek and handed her a mini bouquet of peonies. The flowers complemented the floral orange-and-white crown in the girl's golden curls. As the two walked between the benches of volunteers, friends and family, Rose giggled, her bouquet bouncing like an erratic orchestra conductor's baton. Those baby giggles elicited a lot of clucks and laughs from the guests in the pews.

The butterfly nerves picked up speed in Maureen's tummy as she stood alone, just out of sight of the church's occupants. This was different from her first wedding in so many ways. Unlike her last wedding, her father wasn't here to escort her down the aisle. She tried to bury the thought, will it back to the dark recesses of her mind and think of the reasons this marriage was right. Good. Safe?

Her hand wandered up to her own flowers. The stylist had woven them seamlessly into her hair. To her relief, it seemed like they weren't going anywhere.

The setting, the music, those ancient stones, made her feel like a fairy princess from all the Celtic stories she'd read as a child. If this was to be her fabricated narrative, she wanted the story to have some degree of authenticity, to represent her wildness. Would Xander find that part of her too impractical over time? Would the friendship and passion withstand day-to-day living?

As she made her way to Xander, her bare feet taking in the cool stones along the aisle, her heartbeat roared in her ears. He stood at the altar, a genuine smile radiating from his lips to his eyes. Damn, he was sexy in his suit, with his blue eyes and dark hair. This tall, looming alpha male who'd somehow become such a huge part of her life.

A light breeze carrying the scent of salt and blooming flowers seemed to urge her toward him, tousling her hair slightly, making her feel truly like a water nymph in her dress that mirrored the waves of the ocean, and for a moment, her nerves stilled.

A moment only. Was his smile real? Or was he hiding thoughts of his first wedding? An ache over the loss of his wife? Maureen swallowed hard and pressed forward.

Easton stood next to Xander and shot a quick wink her way. He shifted on his feet, shoulder brushing against a lush green leaf that poked out from the side of the old Spanish-style ruins.

Hibiscus plants and vibrant flowers in sunset hues lined the aisle in homage to their tropical location. Out of the corner of her vision, she saw the smiling faces of the volunteers. They pressed up against each other, hands held to mouths and ears, bowing and flowing like marsh grass. Wisps of words like "She's stunning!" and "Look at the love in his eyes!" caressed her ears. A fairy tale indeed.

Portia smiled at her, holding Rose still on her hip. Her one-shoulder coral gown complementing her fair complexion, the light breeze pushing loose strands of her hair.

Maureen reached the altar, gave herself away, and took her position next to Xander as they both turned to face each other. His hands were warm as they clasped her chilly shaking ones.

Out of the corner of her eyes, her gaze flitted once more to the crowd of people, and she counted those who weren't actually there. Xander's mother had sent an email from Tibet, confirming her inability to attend. She wondered, as the last few notes of the music reverberated, if Xander felt sad about that. Or if, since this was an arrangement, after all, he felt indifferent.

Also missing were his in-laws. Or, his former in-laws. Once Maureen said "I do," their definition would shift. Another way for him to lose more of Terri.

Shoving that thought aside, too, Maureen looked at Xander. He reached for her hand, his touch reassuring and stabilizing. Anchoring. The leap of her pulse only scared her more with fears that she'd let him mean too much to her, too fast.

Rose fussed in Portia's arms, pointing toward Maureen. She lifted Rose from Portia, smiling as the little girl's face lit up, glowing as bright as the sun. Xander touched Maureen's cheek with a gentle stroke of fingertips and emotion in his eyes, a gratitude that she'd allowed his daughter to share in the spotlight of this big moment.

They'd opted to write their own vows rather than go the traditional route and repeat pledges of forever love that would have resembled their first weddings—and also wasn't truthful to their reasoning for this marriage. They'd opted for promises to keep. Honesty.

Maureen had labored over what to say and was relieved that Xander went first. "Maureen, I promise to be here for you. To pledge my every effort to take care of you, to keep you safe, to remind you daily what an incredibly fascinating and alluring and giving woman you are."

"I promise to make you laugh and remember to enjoy life outside the office, to live life to the fullest." She smiled, planting a kiss on Rose's forehead.

The remainder of the ceremony reminded Maureen of a dream. Before she knew it, she locked her lips on his, the strength of his embrace pressing into her. The sparks were there, no question.

Would it be enough?

Flower petals were tossed over them as they left the church to go to the outdoor reception set up just off to the side near the shore. Her toes skimmed over the bright white rocks. Seagulls danced above their heads, circling.

As they moved toward the reception area outdoors, by the ocean, her place of peace, Maureen took in the sounds of the waves crashing, the contained chaos of an unfolding reception. Portia calmly directed people to their tables, smiling, handling the crowds with grace. Maureen appreciated Portia's presence.

Maureen felt like one of the dolls in "It's A Small World"—a smile painfully painted on her face. Volunteers and guests lined up to see her and Xander, offering their congratulations.

All of the smiling and handshaking had her feeling a bit like an animatronic version of herself. The gestures occurring by rote.

Xander and Maureen had split up at the reception to cover more ground to say thank you to their guests. Her hands slid to grasp and hug guest after guest, but her mind focused on that letter she'd gotten in the mail last night.

The lilt of a brogue snapped her attention into focus, her eyes searching for the owner of the voice. Andrea Yeats, the only one of her friends who had been able to fly out for the wedding on such short notice. They'd grown up together, filtering in and out of church together—a dynamic duo.

Andrea raised the glass of merlot to her plump lips, sipping as she nodded at Xander. Shaking her chestnut, curly hair, Andrea lowered her voice, stepping closer to Xander. "I'm so happy for the two of you. You know the old saying there's fault on both sides of a divorce? Well, in their case…she did everything she could to hold that marriage together."

A knot lodged in Maureen's throat. She didn't want to talk about Danny, not this way, and especially not in front of others.

"Andrea—"

But her friend pressed on. "Maureen, you can play nice and be the bigger person, but I don't have to. He was a narcissistic ass. There's no other way around it. He was mentally abusive. He belittled her to death with a thousand paper cuts. It took a lot of courage for her to break away and come here."

"What precipitated the move?" Xander's interest manifested itself in his body language. In the way he leaned on the table.

Maureen had heard enough. Time to take control. "My parents passed away in a ferry accident. Something seemed to click inside me and I moved on. Now, let's move on from this conversation and enjoy the day."

Andrea turned scarlet. Not even her thick, constellation-like freckles could mask the embarrassment gracing Andrea's cheeks. Sheepishly, she wrapped Maureen in a quick hug. "I'm sorry. My mouth ran away with me, love. I just adore you and want to make sure this fella knows how lucky he is to have you." She smiled at them both. "Congratulations. Truly."

With a nervous nod, Andrea excused herself, a predatory swagger in her step as she approached Easton.

With the ocean echoing in the distance at their outdoor reception, Xander slid his arm around her waist and stayed silent, sensing that Maureen didn't want to talk about what had just happened. She was right. This day should be about happiness.

He'd finally claimed her as his own.

Yes, he'd had thoughts of his first wedding today and he would always miss Terri, but Maureen had helped him move forward with his life. Her beautiful, bold personality had shaken him from his fog and brought him back to life again.

He just hated that Andrea had made Maureen so uncomfortable, hurting her with reminders of the past. And, yes, he felt vaguely guilty for prying into her history, but she'd said so little and he wanted to know.

Maureen played with the tips of her curls, fidgeting as her brow furrowed. "Andrea didn't care for my ex-husband." Cool indifference laced her words. She grabbed his hand, pulling him aside, toward the edge of the crowd at the bar.

"Everyone should have a loyal friend." He pulled Maureen close, his hands trailing along the soft exposed skin on her back.

She nodded, chewing on the edge of her bottom lip. "I'm glad she came to visit."

"Are you homesick?" He searched her eyes. Tried to figure out what had her so distant. Learning about the death of her parents... It had changed the way he regarded her. How traumatic that must have been to lose her parents and realize her marriage was a shambles all at once. She'd been truly alone in the world. No wonder she'd made such a large move to start over somewhere fresh without reminders of all she'd lost.

Perhaps she felt their absence acutely today. He felt the absence of his mother like a deep twist of a knife in his gut. And at least she was alive, just not in the picture. He'd missed his dad today, though. The finality of him not being here hurt Xander deeply. He imagined that feeling would intensify if both of his parents were deceased. Guilt stabbed at him now that he'd never thought to ask details about her family, her past. She'd listened to so much he'd shared, drawn him out more than anyone else had been able to.

"Are you homesick?" he repeated since she'd ignored his question the first time. He would be better about listening to her from now on.

"Obviously, I'm trying to stay away from there. I went so far as to marry you, didn't I?" She turned away from him, pulling out of his grasp.

"And a horrible fate that is, right?" He skimmed his knuckles gently across her cheek.

She looked around at the crowd with nervous eyes and linked fingers to draw him behind a palm tree a bit farther from the guests so they wouldn't be interrupted. "Xander, I'm sorry for what I said. That didn't come out right."

He wrapped his arms around her, his back blocking them even further from others in hopes of making it clear they wanted this time alone, if anyone did stumble on them. "You don't need to apologize. I was only teasing." His voice faded to a lull as he realized he really needed to start things off with her by being honest. "What she said about your ex—"

"I told you he walked out on me."

"You didn't tell me he was abusive."

"He never laid a hand on me."

His hand swept over her cheek again, keeping his touch gentle even as anger pulsed through him at the man who'd treated her so poorly. "That's not the only way to abuse someone."

"Andrea talked too much. I'm fine now, happy here, feeling confident and like myself again." A dismal tone edged her voice. She crossed her arms over her chest, shutting down on him.

"You're safe here." He glided his hands down her arms until she relaxed, then pulled her close. "I want you to know that."

"I do." She swallowed hard. "What made you such an expert on emotional abuse?"

"I'm not an expert, but I'm human. And I've dealt with some employee situations…" Her head pushed off his chest to stare at him, eyebrow raised, a bemused smile on her face. He continued, a laugh on his lips. "That sounds lame and impersonal even as I say it. Why don't you tell me about your situation?"

She buried her face back against his chest, shaking her head, a sigh shuddering through her bones. "Andrea said enough. It's in the past. I'm working to restore my life and rebuild my career. Now, can we really stop talking about this? Haven't I said before that I don't want to be one of those individuals who vents nonstop about the ex," she muttered against his shoulder.

"We're married now. This is about making our history." Xander wanted her to feel comfortable talking to him about anything. Everything. The small stuff. The details and stories that shaped her. He wanted her to trust him deeply.

She pulled away from him, her eyes lined with phantom pain. "He was…charming in the beginning. And I fell fast. Looking back, I can see signs I should have paid more attention to."

"Such as?"

"We really should have talked about this before, and maybe this isn't the right time."

He held up a hand, walked over to the waiter and took two champagne flutes, hoping to ease her nerves. His own anger was boiling just below the surface at the man who'd hurt her, but he would keep that under control. For Maureen. He would listen and learn and make sure she had a better marriage this time.

Xander brought the drinks back and guided her farther away from the crowd for even more privacy, finding a bench under a swaying palm in a dim corner.

He passed a drink to Maureen and said, "Maybe we should have talked more, but I would argue we've covered a lot of ground in a week. Now we have plenty of time."

He clinked his glass with hers, and encouraged her to continue.

"My family was so volatile with what you would call a stereotypical Irish temper." She traced along the crystal base, circling with one finger. "Danny kept things light, funny. He was witty. Sarcastic sometimes, but so very witty. I was charmed. We fell fast. Married just as fast. Before long I realized 'light' meant he didn't appreciate deep discussions, especially if that meant addressing a problem. Sarcastic wit turned biting. Hurtful. Anything to shut down a conversation that challenged his perceptions."

Xander could see how much the memories pained her. He'd give anything to make her feel better. "And if avenues for discussion were shut down, I imagine that made it tough to express your frustration or hurt."

She shrugged lightly. "I used to think it was my

fault for being unable to take criticism." She looked at him. "I thought I loved him, or that at least we could find that love again. And then, out of the blue, he told me he wasn't happy, and left. It hurt, but I'm a stronger person now. Much stronger."

"That strength shows. You're strong and compassionate." He met her honesty with his own. He had seen firsthand how deeply Maureen cared for those around her…how much more so she must have felt for a man she'd been in love with. Those feelings didn't just erode overnight. The death of a marriage—for good reasons and bad ones—still had consequences in the heart.

"Thank you." Tears pushed at her eyes.

He pulled her closer, needing to show he cared.

"The breakdown of a marriage is tragic." The end of love hurt. By death or divorce. He knew that too damn well.

"But I truly am better off."

"I believe you are." He kissed her cheek. Her nose. Her lips. She sighed, falling into him more before continuing to speak.

"It just galls me that I didn't see the truth sooner. That made me doubt myself for a very long time."

"And now?"

"I'm doing better."

"Getting married again must have been difficult for you," he said, his hands roving over her arms.

"But this isn't about love. That gives me a level of emotional protection."

Her words felt like a wall coming between them.

He didn't have time to process that. Not now. Easton and Portia approached them.

"It's showtime." Easton's words slurred slightly.

Portia laughed, adjusting her one shoulder strap. "What he is trying to say is that it's time for us to send you lovebirds off."

She gestured to the crowd, which parted like the Red Sea, leading to a stretch beach buggy with a chauffeur waiting to take them to a cabana on Key Largo for their first night as man and wife before departing to Sicily for a proper honeymoon. All the trappings of romance intact.

After watching the chauffeur disappear down the thin, sandy lane, Maureen turned to face Xander. Her husband.

God, how strange that word felt. This day had been surreal enough without Andrea showing up and eliciting that whole conversation about Danny that Maureen just wasn't ready to have yet.

And then there was the job offer still looming over her that she hadn't told Xander about. Not that it mattered now. She wasn't going to take it. But she should tell him.

Before she had time to process all the tumult of the day, much less their new roles, Xander swept her off her feet. Literally.

Six hours as man and wife. She knew him as a boss. A friend. A lover. But this? This was…beyond anything she would have considered happening.

Moonlight bathed them in silver as he carried her

toward the door of the cabana. The ocean provided the soundtrack—a mounting sound of waves and night birds.

Each step up to the cabana caused him to draw her closer, the scent of sandalwood intoxicating her. Over the threshold and into the cabana, he took her.

Xander let her slide out of his arms, her bare feet touching the grain of the wood. He pushed her gently against the wall, kissing her deeply.

She wanted more of him. Angling into his kiss, she pushed farther. He pressed his hand on her hip, sending an electric pulse through her limbs.

She raised a hand to his jawline. He leaned into it for a moment, her fingers taking in the way his chin curved. His head tilted to the table at the center of the living room.

She followed his gaze, settling on the baskets filled with gifts—a collection of jasmine and vanilla massage oils, lotions and rainbow-colored condoms. A gift from Easton, according to the tag.

A bucket filled with ice and champagne took position to the left. Another basket brimmed with chocolates and dried fruits.

Platters of exotic cheeses, grapes, chocolate-dipped strawberries and crackers covered the remainder of the table. True decadent indulgence.

Xander picked up a chocolate-covered strawberry and fed it to her. Eyes on him still, she bit down into the fruit, enjoying the contrast of bitter dark chocolate and sweet strawberry. He discarded the top of the strawberry, brushing her top lip with his thumb before grabbing one of the oils and a condom from the basket.

"Coming?" His question came out breathy. She nodded, following him to the bedroom.

Rose petals speckled the ground and the bed. He kissed her hand, traced the edge of her collarbone, sending shivers down her spine. Helped her out of the gown.

"Let me spoil you. Pamper you." He gestured to the bed.

"You're too kind," she mumbled, climbing onto the silken sheets. He rubbed the oil between his hands and then pressed into her shoulders.

"Relax, Maureen. There's no reason to be so tense." He worked on her shoulders, releasing the tension with every stroke. "Everything's going to be okay. More than okay."

He began kissing her neck, back, hip. She turned over to face him, propping herself up on her forearms to kiss him.

Xander pushed her back down, hand grazing her thigh. His mouth sought hers, body pressed against hers. Urgency entered with his tongue. Roving hands teased her nipples.

Her hand wrapped around the length of him, stroking, caressing, her thumb rubbing along the tip of him until he growled with the intense pleasure of just how perfectly she seemed to know how to move him.

His desire for her grew with each movement. She became slick with feminine want. Their normal fire and frenzy changed tonight, replaced with a calm burn. A steady burn.

He kept kissing her. Her hands pulled him closer, raking lightly down his back. Her nails scored his skin ever so lightly, just enough to relay her desire.

Xander eased inside her, each thrust slow and deep as his eyes held hers. Her hips rocked against his, every move of their bodies releasing the sweet scent of the shared fruit mixed with a growing perspiration of need. Building desire. She slid her heels up the backs of his calves, higher still until her legs locked around his waist.

The urgent need to find completion built inside him, along with the realization that once—hell, twelve times or more—wouldn't be enough.

The need was becoming greater with each passing day. The sweet clasp of her body around his sent his pulse pounding in his ears, his heart pounding against his chest. His whole body throbbed from want of her. Maureen. Her name echoed in his mind again and again.

Even while he burned to reach completion, still he took them to the edge—holding back then pushing her closer until she was wild with need. He reveled in the flush of desire spreading over her flesh, attesting to her pleasure. Her hands twisting in the sheets and rose petals alike until he brought her to a crashing release. His final deep thrust and hoarse shout made it clear he'd followed her over that edge with every bit as much bliss, their bodies connected as they rolled to their sides, panting.

* * *

As their breathing slowed to a more even pace, chests rising and falling in time together, her heart grew heavy. All of the complications of this arrangement came crashing down on her. With a weighty realization. She loved him.

She loved Xander.

And what scared her in the pit of her stomach was that even though he cared for her, even though she suspected he might one day come to love her, he would never care for her as much as he'd loved Terri. The thought rocked her.

"When was the last time you went stargazing?" he asked, kissing her.

Hesitancy flooded her. "Um. Ages ago."

"Let's change that." He handed her a silk robe out of the closet and put his clothes back on. Xander disappeared for a moment, returning with the basket full of chocolates and dried fruit in hand.

"Come with me." He opened the balcony door of the cabana. She followed, wrapping the silk against her bare skin, taking in the mesh of starred horizon and cool ocean, her revelation knotting in her stomach.

On the porch there were two oversize chairs. Maureen sank into one and Xander reached for her hand, staring at her with dreamy eyes. Melting her heart a little bit more. The world unbalancing.

Until a masculine brogue cut through the air.

"I've come for my wife."

Ice chilled her blood. She didn't even have to look over her shoulder to know.

Andrea wasn't the only person from her past to have come to the States today.

Danny had arrived.

Twelve

Maureen went rigid next to Xander. She'd inhaled sharply, eyes falling in the direction of the voice.

In the muted light of moon and stars, the form of a somewhat muscular man manifested. He approached them, features coming into focus with every step.

Danny.

Maureen's ex. Fists tightened, more than ready to slam the guy's teeth through his face if it became necessary. The urge to send Maureen inside wailed in Xander's head. Standing up from the chair, he looked down at the man, unwilling to resort to violence unless absolutely necessary.

Damn, but he hoped it would be necessary.

Danny's bronzed, buzzed hair practically glowed

in the moonlight. Xander noticed how his handsome face seemed to be chiseled by bitterness.

How in the world had he found them? For the last two years Maureen had flown under the radar. He racked his brain. No matter what, he'd make sure she was safe. That thought coursed through his mind on full-blast.

"What are you doing here? And, more important, who the hell do you think you are to call yourself my husband?" Maureen lobbed pure fire at him, blazing and glorious.

"Fine, ex-husband. But I've come here to win you back, love. I miss you." His brogue was thick and deep. But Xander thought the man's swagger was a bit cartoonish, as if he was trying to put on some kind of machismo show.

Through clenched teeth, Xander said tightly, leaving no room for doubt, "She's not just engaged. We got married today."

"I'm too late?" Shock pushed his mouth into a faux grin dripping with malice. He took a few steps closer. "I heard she was engaged and the wedding was soon, so I came running. But married? Already? I screwed up the time change or something, I had plans for—"

The jackass had actually planned to burst into their wedding? Xander's eyes narrowed. "How did you even know about the engagement?"

Maureen sighed. "Andrea. Tossing it in your face that I've rebuilt my life."

Danny sneered. "She enjoyed every minute of crowing over that."

Xander put a protective arm around Maureen, damned determined she wouldn't be facing this demeaning jerk alone. "I'm her husband. She and I got married." He held up her hand to show off her ring. "It's official. Ring, certificate and all."

Danny whistled lowly, his attention narrowed on Maureen. "That is quite a rock. You landed a big fish. No wonder you don't want me."

Maureen stepped forward, her chin tipped high and proud. Strong. "Danny, I didn't want you before. I don't want you now. And the feeling was mutual, so I have no idea what you're doing here. I believe it's best you state your business and go off somewhere to sightsee or something."

Xander tucked her back at his side. Even knowing she could handle herself, he didn't want her to think she had to do this alone. He wanted to support her, to protect her. To let her know how amazing she was and how undeserving of this kind of jerk show. "Clearly this is a surprise to you, but this is how things are. Now, if you'll kindly leave—"

Danny shook his head, tapping his chin. "Something's fishy and I'm not going anywhere until I get some answers to—"

Glancing at Maureen, Xander noted the way her body had begun to shake with anger. Distress marred her face, but she wasn't backing down. Damn it, she didn't have to face this alone. No one, especially not Danny, would ever harass Maureen. Not while he was around. "You're on private property. You will only be allowed to stay if my *wife* wants you to be here." He turned to her and cocked an eyebrow. "Maureen?"

She shook her head.

Xander shrugged. "It's final, then. Your visit is done. If you wish to speak with my wife, you may, of course, call, or better yet, send a certified letter."

Danny's voice became more agitated, louder. "But I'm the one that left—"

Standing her ground, Maureen stared him down with strength and fire in her eyes. "And you'll be leaving now. Having you out of my life is a blessing. I moved forward. I have an amazing job." She leaned closer to Xander. "And a wonderful husband. You and I no longer have any connection. So please, don't contact me again."

A calculating look entered Danny's steely eyes as his gaze moved from Maureen to Xander and back again, a laugh lodged in his throat. "Your job... And this is your boss." A slow, smarmy smile ticked at the corners of his mouth. "Convenient you got married right before you had to come home. Wasn't that job offer you got from the university big enough for you?"

Xander took him by the arm. "This discussion is over. I'm calling security."

With admirable speed, Don, still wearing his suit from attending the wedding, came to pick Danny up. Xander helped Don secure the man in the car, closed the door and watched him drive away. Satisfied to see him gone. And return to Maureen.

He wanted to make sure Maureen was safe. And not just tonight. But forever. He wanted to shield her as best he could. Because he…because he loved her. Truly and deeply loved her. It took nothing away from what he'd felt for Terri. In fact, Terri had taught him to love and he knew now that the greatest gift he could give her was to let love into his heart again.

And without question, he loved Maureen every bit as deeply as any love he'd ever felt before.

Tears cascaded down Maureen's fair cheeks. She shook uncontrollably, hands wrapping around herself. "I feel awful. He all but said we married for my green card and he's right."

Xander touched her lips then thumbed away her tears. "I needed a mother for my child to ensure she stays with me."

"Great. We pulled a fast one on the courts twice."

"Do you believe Rose is where she belongs?"

"Absolutely."

"Are you happier married to me than you were to him?"

"That's not even a fair question. I could be happier married to just about anyone."

"Then are you happy here, in the house…" He leaned closer. "In my bed." He touched her mouth again. "You don't even need to answer that. I heard your joy loud and clear that night before we stepped out on the porch."

Her cheeks flushed. "Loudly?"

"Delightfully so. And I look forward to making that happen again and again."

A part of the conversation with Danny gnawed at him. She seemed calm now, but he had to ask, had to know if she was making arrangements to leave him. "So tell me what he meant about that big job offer at the university."

She shook her head. "There's nothing to discuss."

"But it's a big deal," he pressed, hoping to get something out of her.

She shrugged.

His body chilled all the way to his soul. "Are you taking it?"

"No," she insisted quickly. "Of course not."

Then he asked the question he had to know. "If the job had been offered earlier this week, would you have accepted it?"

She looked away quickly. Too quickly for his liking. "Uh, Xander, I should double-check my suitcase for our trip."

He clasped her elbow gently. "Are you sure you still want to travel after the upset you've just had?"

She finally met his eyes. "The fact that you're asking offers the answer already. Maybe it's best that we delay any honeymoon plans."

"Is that what you really want? No honeymoon? Not even an attempt at starting this marriage off on a positive note?"

Her eyebrows shot up. "This is already nowhere close to a positive note. I think we both need to stop this discussion before we say something that can't be taken back. This is a marriage of convenience. Let's not lose sight of that."

She tugged her arm free and walked away, closing the door with a finality that echoed to his toes. He was losing her before he'd even fully had her.

Not her, too. He couldn't lose another wife. He couldn't go through that again in any way.

He couldn't lose Maureen.

A familiar sound buzzed in his pocket. Easton's ringtone. Of course.

He fished the phone out of his pocket, sliding to accept the call.

"This is your best-man courtesy call. Your jet is fueled and ready for the Lourdes party of two first thing in the morning."

"Forget it. Cancel the flight. Maureen and I had a disagreement." He sank onto a chair, running his free hand through his thick hair. Wondering how he'd gotten to this place so quickly. He didn't want to lose her.

"A fight over what, if you don't mind my asking?" Easton sighed. "You didn't do something dumbass like murmur your first wife's name during sex…"

"God, no. Thanks for the vote of confidence," he quipped back with a levity he was far from feeling.

"But you still love Terri." His brother's question was more of a statement.

"I will always love her." There would never be a moment where he'd be able to stop those feelings. But he now knew that he had a bigger capacity for love than he'd imagined.

"Of course you will."

"I'm not sure how another woman would feel about that," Xander admitted.

"If she were alive today you would still be married."

"We would." Xander snagged a grape from the fruit basket and rolled it between his fingers.

"Of course you would. But you also need to ask yourself honestly…will you be able to love another woman as much as you loved her? Because no woman wants to be second best."

Easton's tone was level but firm. Perhaps this was what Easton had been hinting at when he'd promised to beat Xander's ass if he hurt her. Because Maureen, a woman whose past marriage had been filled with emotional games, had developed a callus around her heart. She'd become accustomed to not being enough.

And just making that connection—realizing that he had, however unwittingly, treated her the same way as that ass of an ex-husband he'd met tonight—made Xander furious with himself.

Having heard every damn thing he needed to, Xander ended the call, understood with crystal clarity that he needed to follow after her. Now.

Tossing the grape into the waste can, he charged through the cabana to find her sitting on the overstuffed pale peach chair, her delicate legs tucked beneath her. Palm to chin, she gazed absently into space. Years of pain were written in her posture. The letter from the university hung limply in her hands.

"I don't know how much I have inside left to give. But I'm trying, Maureen. I want this to work between us. I want to give it a real try. The question is—" he tapped the letter "—do you?"

Her hesitation, her lack of an answer, was all he needed. Whatever she felt for him, for his daughter, for this island, didn't come close to what he felt for her. But then, when had she been shown how deeply a man could love a woman? Certainly not by that jackass she'd been married to the first time.

She wrapped her arms tightly around herself. "I think it's best we cancel the honeymoon and go back to the house."

Watching her close him out, Xander realized that he could lose her, really lose her. Forever, in fact, if he didn't put his heart on the line and let her know how much she meant to him.

Rattled.

Unsettled.

The feelings coalesced inside her, becoming a pressure system of anxiety. She'd known this wasn't at all the right time to travel and maybe some of that had to do with the shock of seeing Danny again. She knew Xander was a far better man. But that didn't mean he loved her and it didn't change the fact that they'd entered this marriage for convenience's sake only.

So Sicily? Now? No. She wouldn't have been able to enjoy herself or their time together.

She'd told Xander they should go back to the house and rethink their plans.

They'd told the volunteers and family she had a sinus infection and couldn't fly. Not a tough sell since her sinuses were stuffed after she'd cried her eyes out in the shower.

But with work covered, she had nothing to do, so she'd sought comfort in playing with Rose at the beach. They sat together on a blanket with a pile of blocks.

Rose sat in her lap, humming a made-up tune that seemed to mimic the sounds of the nearby parrots. A call-and-response of innocence and wonder.

This little girl had quickly taken up residence in her heart. Made her want to stay.

Scooting out of her lap, Rose picked up the building blocks and began stacking them together. Smiling back at Maureen, still singing her little ditty.

Handing over a block, Rose giggled. "Yooouuu." Her bell-like voice was small and sweet.

Maureen stacked her yellow block on Rose's green one. The little girl clapped, bobbing her head from side to side. Clearly amused and satisfied by the progress they'd made.

But Maureen didn't share in the toddler's delight. The fight with Xander had left her shaken and heartsick. When she'd seen Danny, standing there in the moonlight, the life she'd fled crashed back around her.

All the strength and healing fell away in that moment. She knew Danny didn't care about her one damn bit. He'd showed up only to unsettle her. To beat her back down. Just another move in his emotionally abusive chess game.

He'd been forcibly removed from the property and given a restraining order.

But the damage to Maureen had already been done. Before he'd left her, she'd become unsure of her place and worth. Those feelings returned, fully visible, in the heated exchange with Xander.

Xander. Whom she loved.

That thought scared her, rendering her completely vulnerable. The jumble of insecurities stilled her tongue when she should have spoken up.

Of course she wanted to stay. Wanted to be in Rose's life. And Xander's.

The block tower had grown quite high and, with a devilish look in her eye, Rose pushed on the middle pieces. The whole thing tumbled, eliciting peals of laughter from Rose.

How appropriate.

But then Rose began to build the tower again. Maureen admired her tenacity. Her willingness to simply start again.

Handing over a green block, Maureen said, "Parrot."

Rose took the block, nodding. She picked up a yellow one, handing it to Maureen. "Puppy."

"That's right, love," Maureen said softly.

A rustle of sand caused Maureen to turn around. Xander approached, plopping down on the beach blanket next to them. He was dressed in khaki shorts and an old white T-shirt, and there was something decidedly off about him. His face was tense, his eyes sad. "We need to talk."

Her stomach flip-flopped with a sense of dread. "Should I take Rose back to the house?"

He shook his head. "If you don't mind, she's happy. Let's let her keep playing."

"Okay, then. What did you want to say?"

He tossed a block from hand to hand. "I had a talk with my brother. He has a brilliant mind and some damn good insights, ones I always listen to when I remind myself that I should do more listening."

"Were you always close?" Maureen asked, watching the movements in his eyes. "You don't talk much now, so it's tough to tell."

"We're both so wrapped up in our work there isn't as much time. We work all hours. We've talked more in my time here than… God, in I don't know how long." His hand went to his hair, a shrug in his shoulders.

"And when you were children?"

"Our parents were very into letting us learn through experience."

The statement gave her pause. "What do you mean?"

"They weren't helicopter parents, other than the fact they strapped us into helicopters at a young age to tour the Andes. We were homeschooled for real, except home was around the world."

A bohemian lifestyle. It explained so much about Easton's approach. Even the way he talked to people. "That sounds like your brother's style, but not so much yours."

"Are you insinuating I'm uptight?" Arms immediately crossed over his chest.

Rose hummed louder, chanting random words into her melody. Maureen handed the baby another block, which she took as fast as a snapping turtle.

"Not by a long shot. You're sexy and exciting. But you're a businessman and a family man. Not a hippie veterinarian." And, honestly, she enjoyed that about him. He was her naturally occurring counterweight in so many ways.

"I realized that fast and made my own plans accordingly."

"What kind of plans?" Maureen added a block to Rose's tower. Rose high-fived her, then toppled the tower.

"Lots of plans, some better than others. I planned to go to college and get my business degree to start my own company. My brother was clear he wanted to be an exotic animal veterinarian."

"Which you both did. What were some of your other boyhood plans?" In the span of five minutes, some of the harshness of the morning ebbed away. She felt as though, for the first time, he trusted her with the vulnerable bits of his life. Maureen wanted him to keep sharing.

"We decided to catch the biggest fish for a local contest. The grand prize was five thousand dollars."

"Wow, that's a lot of money for a fish." She knew

fishing contests drew a lot of attention, but hadn't really understood the appeal.

"It was for the serious fishermen, but we had big dreams and bigger egos. We were certain we could make it happen."

"And did you?" Resting her face on her palm, she leaned forward.

He waved, a smile tugging at his lips. A bit of the Xander she knew and loved peeking through. "Wait for the story. Give it time to breathe."

"You're seriously telling me to slow down and relax? Mr. Fast-Paced Executive?"

"I'm learning. Anyhow, I built the boat. My brother researched the fishing channels. I adapted the dynamics of the craft to his calculations." He picked up a block, handing it to Rose.

"How did the competition turn out?"

"We caught the most fish, but not the biggest. We lost by two ounces."

"Seriously? Only two ounces? That must have been a huge fish." The tropical fish of Florida astounded her. So different from the fish in the streams and lakes of Ireland, so vibrant and mammoth.

"We ate well. We filled the freezer with the extra, then started a campfire to grill the rest for Mom and Dad by suppertime." He gestured with his hands, as if drawing that freezer back to the present.

She tried to picture a younger Easton and Xander hauling in the fish. The image made her laugh.

"That's really thoughtful."

"Um, Mom turned white and passed out and Dad

gave us one helluva lecture about going out on the water without an adult."

"How old were you?"

"Ten and eleven." That sly smile returned. He looked at her sidelong, his blue eyes complementing the state of the sky. Piercing and intoxicating.

"What did they think the boat you'd been building was for?"

"They assumed it would be for local villagers on our latest family expedition. And it was. Once we finished with it."

She nodded, thinking she understood. But she wanted clarity. Time to be brave. "Where were you going with that story just now?"

"I was making a couple of points, really. The first point, the less pertinent one, is that for a long time I thought you and my brother might be an item because you have so much in common."

Shock rippled through her, then amusement. A laugh of disbelief snorted free. "Me? And Easton? Seriously?"

He nodded.

"Clearly you realized that's not the case at all. No disrespect to your brother. He's a brilliant veterinarian, but he's a friend and a work companion. Nothing more."

"Okay, I believe you."

She took the block from his hand, reading hesitancy in his eyes. "But what?"

"He's the sort of person you would be with at that university job, the world you're from." He paused, inhaling deeply before continuing. "Are you taking the job?"

"No," she said without hesitation. "Of course not. We made promises to each other."

His hand fell to rest on his daughter's head, his eyes still searching Maureen's. "So you're staying because of Rose? So she doesn't risk a custody battle?"

And in a flash she realized, holy hell, he was every bit as insecure as she was when it came to giving his heart again. She lifted his hand from Rose's head, linked fingers with his and went out on the biggest limb of her life. "I'm staying because of you and what's happening between us. I hope you believe me."

His throat moved in a long swallow and he squeezed her hand. "Obviously I haven't been thinking with the clearest of minds for a while, not since Terri's death. I will always love her, but I hope you understand that doesn't mean I can't fall in love with another woman just as deeply."

Her heart leaped at his words, at his implication. Could it be? Her hearing intensified, causing her to lean closer, hand touching his thigh.

"Once I realized how close I was to losing you, to your work visa expiring and your leaving for Ireland, I acted fast. Just like with the boat, I knew on some level what had to be done."

"But your in-laws? They were a threat—"

He waved a hand dismissively. "They're coming around, I believe. They love Rose, but they don't want to be parents again. They already sent flowers this morning with a congratulations and a request to come for a lunch visit to discuss how to be helpful, involved grandparents." He tapped his temple. "On some level, I knew they would see reason."

"But I didn't." She eyed him. "You manipulated me?"

"I did what I needed to in order to make you stay. To give us this chance at a life together, because, Maureen, I love you. If we waited here while someone counted every grain of sand on the beach, there wouldn't be enough time to explain how much you mean to me. And if you'll give me a chance, I'll prove it to you and, hopefully, with time, you'll come to love me in return."

Relief coursed through her as she saw the truth in his eyes. She'd spent so long telling herself not to believe in the fairy tale, but maybe it wasn't a fairy tale. The truth had been building all along and she'd been so worried about being hurt again, she hadn't allowed herself to see it.

She caressed his face. "How beautifully lucky for us that I already am in love with you."

Urgency filled her. She'd found courage again. Leaning in to kiss him, she angled her head below his. A tender kiss transferring from her lips to his. Electricity melded with comfort, the kiss feeling like a long-overdue homecoming.

His hand braced her chin, fingers soft.

Maureen felt a smaller hand touch her cheek three times. They broke the kiss to see Rose beaming at them. She kissed Maureen's cheek, then Xander's. A ripple of laughter passed between them all. Everything settling into place. Together.

Xander scooped up his daughter and wrapped an arm around his wife's waist. "What do you say we put Rose down for a nap and we make new honeymoon plans? Together."

She leaned against his shoulder, her arm sliding around his waist, as well. "I like the sound of that, husband. Very much."

* * * * *

*If you liked this story of a billionaire dad tamed
by the love of the right woman,
pick up these other novels from*
USA TODAY *bestselling author*
Catherine Mann

*YULETIDE BABY SURPRISE
FOR THE SAKE OF THEIR SON
PREGNANT BY THE COWBOY CEO
A CHRISTMAS BABY SURPRISE
HIS PREGNANT PRINCESS BRIDE*

Available now from Harlequin Desire!

* * *

And don't miss the next BILLIONAIRES
AND BABIES *story*
*THE BLACK SHEEP'S SECRET CHILD
by Cat Schield
Available October 2016!*

* * *

*If you're on Twitter, tell us what you think
of Harlequin Desire! #harlequindesire*

REQUEST YOUR FREE BOOKS!
2 FREE NOVELS PLUS 2 FREE GIFTS!

HARLEQUIN®

Desire

ALWAYS POWERFUL, PASSIONATE AND PROVOCATIVE

YES! Please send me 2 FREE Harlequin® Desire novels and my 2 FREE gifts (gifts are worth about $10). After receiving them, if I don't wish to receive any more books, I can return the shipping statement marked "cancel." If I don't cancel, I will receive 6 brand-new novels every month and be billed just $4.55 per book in the U.S. or $5.24 per book in Canada. That's a savings of at least 13% off the cover price! It's quite a bargain! Shipping and handling is just 50¢ per book in the U.S. and 75¢ per book in Canada.* I understand that accepting the 2 free books and gifts places me under no obligation to buy anything. I can always return a shipment and cancel at any time. Even if I never buy another book, the two free books and gifts are mine to keep forever.

225/326 HDN GH2P

Name	(PLEASE PRINT)	
Address		Apt. #
City	State/Prov.	Zip/Postal Code

Signature (if under 18, a parent or guardian must sign)

Mail to the **Reader Service:**
IN U.S.A.: P.O. Box 1867, Buffalo, NY 14240-1867
IN CANADA: P.O. Box 609, Fort Erie, Ontario L2A 5X3

Want to try two free books from another line?
Call 1-800-873-8635 or visit www.ReaderService.com.

Gavin grabbed his duffel from the truck. He tilted his
Stetson back on his head and looked at the car parked
in front of his grandmother's guest cottage. Gavin hoped
his grandmother hadn't extended an invitation for that
professor to stay on their property as well as dig on their
land. He didn't want anyone taking advantage of his
family.

He'd taken one step onto the porch when the front
door swung open and his grandmother walked out. She
was smiling, and when she opened her arms, he dropped
his duffel bag and walked straight into the hug awaiting
him.

"Welcome home, Gavin," she said. "I didn't expect
you for a few months yet. Did everything go okay?"

He smiled. She always asked him the same thing,
knowing full well that because of the classified nature
of his job as a SEAL, he couldn't tell her anything.
"Yes, Gramma Mel, everything went okay. I'm back
because—"

He blinked, not sure he was seeing straight. A woman stood in the doorway, but she wasn't just *some* woman. She had to be the most gorgeous woman he'd ever seen. Hell, she looked like everything he'd ever fantasized a woman to be, even while fully clothed in jeans and a pullover sweater.

Gavin studied her features, trying to figure out what had him spellbound. Was it the caramel-colored skin, dark chocolate eyes, dimpled cheeks, button nose or well-defined, kissable lips? Maybe every single thing.

Not waiting for his grandmother to make introductions, his mouth eased into a smile. He reached out his hand and said, "Hello, I'm Gavin."

The moment their hands touched, a jolt of desire shot through his body. Nothing like this had ever happened to him before. From the expression that flashed in her eyes, he knew she felt it, as well.

"It's nice meeting you, Gavin," she said softly. "Layla Harris."

Harris? His aroused senses suddenly screeched to a stop. Did she say *Harris*? Was Layla related to this Professor Harris? Was she part of the excavation team?

Now he had even more questions, and he was determined to get some answers.

Don't miss
THE RANCHER RETURNS
by New York Times *bestselling author Brenda Jackson,*
available October 2016 wherever
Harlequin® Desire books and ebooks are sold.

www.Harlequin.com

Whatever You're Into... Passionate Reads

Looking for more passionate reads from Harlequin®?
Fear not! Harlequin® Presents, Harlequin® Desire and
Harlequin® Blaze offer you irresistible romance stories
featuring powerful heroes.

◆HARLEQUIN *Presents*.

Do you want alpha males, decadent glamour and jet-set
lifestyles? Step into the sensational, sophisticated world of
Harlequin® Presents, where sinfully tempting heroes ignite a
fierce and wickedly irresistible passion!

◆HARLEQUIN *Desire*

Harlequin® Desire novels are powerful, passionate and
provocative contemporary romances set against a backdrop of
wealth, privilege and sweeping family saga. Alpha heroes with
a soft side meet strong-willed but vulnerable heroines amid a
dramatic world of divided loyalties, high-stakes conflict and
intense emotion.

◆HARLEQUIN *Blaze*

Harlequin® Blaze stories sizzle with strong heroines and
irresistible heroes playing the game of modern love and lust.
They're fun, sexy and always steamy.

Be sure to check out our full selection of books
within each series every month!

www.Harlequin.com

HPASSION2016